The Lizards of Palm Beach

The Lizards of Palm Beach
A Novel

Bruce McDougall

Owl Canyon Press

First Edition, 2021
All Rights Reserved
Library of Congress Cataloging-in-Publication Data

McDougall, Bruce
The Lizards of Palm Beach —1st ed.
p. cm.
ISBN: 978-1-952085-04-8
Library of Congress Control Number: 2020945726

Owl Canyon Press
Boulder, Colorado

Dedication:

To Jan, mia regazza,
and
To SRD & JJD, with thanks

"Clearly money has something to do with life."
Philip Larkin

PROLOGUE

On the night that Rollo Barnes and I met at the at the M2 Gallery, he was wearing brown suit pants, snakeskin cowboy boots and a long-sleeved yellow shirt made of some space-age material that would have melted in a microwave. His grey hair was combed back from his high tanned forehead and fastened in a ponytail. I was tempted to take his picture, but it wouldn't have done either of us any good to run it in the paper. Rollo doesn't need to prove his place in the Palm Beach pecking order, and I needed the space to run a photo of someone who did.

Barnes and I get together about twice a month, sometimes at a gallery, sometimes at a bar, but always to continue our ongoing argument about wealth. Like many people, Barnes thinks wealthy people should be penalized for having so much money. That way, you could discourage people who have more money than imagination from turning nice empty spaces into theme parks like Palm Beach.

Barnes's point of view seems ironic to me. He's old money. One of his uncles was an ambassador to England. His grandfather founded Dreyfus Barnes on Wall Street around the beginning of the last century. His great-grandfather owned most of the iron-ore deposits around Lake Superior and sold them to Andrew Carnegie and U.S. Steel. Dreyfus Barnes survived the Great Depression and by the nineteen-sixties was one of the more established investment banks in the world. These days, they say it's too big to fail. There are people in Palm Beach who believe that about themselves.

Barnes's father married a Phipps. They had two children together. Rollo was the second, but by the time he was born, his father had moved on to another wife. Rollo's mother was nobody special. Who knows why they named their kid Rollo? Maybe his mother liked chocolates with caramel filling. I doubt if she'd ever heard of Graham Greene or his character, Rollo Martins. Barnes is in his sixties now. He's still tall, and he looks fit, but he doesn't exercise much outside the bedroom. He smokes a lot, and he likes fast cars and good Scotch. I don't think he's worked a day in his life, which probably explains why he doesn't try to impress the world with his money. Money is something that happened to him, like brown eyes or big feet.

I keep telling Barnes that wealth isn't a zero-sum game. If you take five dollars from a wealthy person, a poor person won't become five dollars richer. I tell him that the world needs more wealthy people, not fewer, especially extravagant ones like the people who live in Palm Beach, because they don't hoard their money, they spend it. If you have something they want, they'll buy it from you. That's the way the world works these days. "Where would you rather live?" I ask him. "In a kingdom like Jordan, where one person controls all the wealth? Or in a country like this, where there are hundreds of millionaires, and anyone can get rich?"

My argument seems as ironic as Barnes's, since I don't have any money at all. But that's Palm Beach for you. It's a funny place, tucked into the Atlantic coastline, half-way down the Florida peninsula, where no one in his right mind would live if it weren't for the palm trees and the wealth. The trees grew in the nineteenth century from coconuts that washed onto shore from a shipwrecked freighter. The money arrived later.

Like one of the legendary coconuts, I washed up in Palm Beach about eight years ago, when I landed a job with the *Spectator*. The paper's a nice little weekly money-maker that runs flattering photos of rich people that don't draw attention to their flaws, cosmetic or otherwise. It's owned by a man named Polosi, who made a fortune in the cheese business in Chicago and doesn't stick his nose into my business as long as we make a profit and never refer to the Kennedys, whom he despises. In return for an annual salary that wouldn't cover the cost of a tank of gas in one of our subscribers' private jets, I watch the way that people live in Palm Beach, listen to what they say and write it down without interrupting them when they grace me with their gilded wisdom. Sometimes I write down what they don't say, as well, but I've kept that to myself until now.

For the last eight years, I've watched the way money affects people. Sometimes it brings out the best in them. They endow academic chairs, support theaters and art galleries, sponsor athletes, build hospitals and libraries. Once in a while, they do this anonymously, with true generosity in their hearts. But sometimes wealth makes people careless, arrogant and sloppy. It's not entirely their fault. People adjust to their community. They become accustomed to its nuances and accommodate themselves to behavior that the rest of us might find offensive. Live long enough with headhunters in New Guinea and eventually you'll see nothing peculiar about mounting someone's skull on a pole. Live long enough in Palm Beach, and you won't think twice about paying sixty thousand dollars for a handbag and firing your maid for talking to you about her sick child.

Some rich people equate money with intelligence, and they like to think they have more of it than I do. I use my intelligence to convince myself that I don't care what they think. Like most people on the planet, I scrape by from one day to the next on money that I earn by selling my limited talents to the highest bidder. I play the game just like everyone else. Very few of us can afford not to put a price on his time, talent or integrity. This doesn't bother me much. We all have to find a way to live in the world into which we're born. Some people sell their bodies, some people sell their souls, but I don't know many people who can afford not to sell themselves in one way or another. With few exceptions, all of us are hookers. It's the world we live in.

Palm Beach attracts top-drawer hookers, especially during The Season. Between November and April, the place becomes a gulag of sybaritic narcissism, plastic surgery, opulence and questionable taste. That's when rich people in Palm Beach let down their hair transplants: the men abandon their tailored suits for Versace jeans and Gucci loafers without socks; the women wear pastel cashmere sweaters and Loro Piana shorts and study each other's jaw lines for the tell-tale signs of a scalpel's incision. The local pet shop sells diamond-studded dog collars and monogrammed pillows for Chihuahuas. Restaurants like Ta-boo and Bice serve mediocre food at inflated prices and compete to hire the best-looking, beach-bronzed valets to fetch their customers' Bentleys. It's cottage country for people who pay other people to get their hands dirty, but it has the same air of transience and impermanence as any other resort town. There's no hospital, no funeral home and no cemetery in Palm Beach, and the only doctors are cosmetic dentists and dermatologists on vacation from Duluth or Cleveland. This is a town of insiders, where the residents delight in small ironies. A women's clothing shop on Worth Avenue is called Eye of the Needle. A street running north from The Everglades Club is called Cocoanut Road, with an a, because the developer of the street didn't know how to spell. He was allowed to spell the name the way he wanted, because he was also the mayor.

The Season ends when the temperature starts to rise. By April, the mansions stand empty behind their tall ficus hedges. Their owners have moved on to Mayfair or Biarritz or some other center of regimented pleasure where rich people can be rich together. The only people who stay in town are over-the-hill gigolos who have nowhere else to go and no one to take them anywhere and the semi-wealthy widows of deceased auto-parts manufacturers from Ohio, surviving on a meager inheritance and the fumes of their husbands' life insurance policies. They live in cramped little condos near the grocery store and pass the time by walking on the beach or roaming the air-conditioned aisles of Publix in their tennis skirts and Tod's driving shoes, chatting with strangers and filling their grocery carts with day-old bread and rotting bananas. To save money on food, they go to gallery openings, where they can get a glass of cheap wine and a few slivers of smoked salmon on a piece of dry toast in exchange for spending one more hour of their lives in a state of vertical semi-consciousness. They may admire the art, but they can't afford to buy it, not at the inflated prices that galleries charge in Palm Beach.

I was attending one of these openings at a gallery on Worth Avenue called M2, when I bumped into Rollo Barnes. I was surprised to see him there.

I'd just leaned forward to examine one of the sculptures on display. It had taken my breath away although I didn't realize that I'd stopped breathing until Barnes sidled over to stand beside me.

"Like it?" said Rollo.

"I can't take my eyes off it," I said.

"And in the M2 Gallery, no less," said Rollo. "The last place you'd expect to find genuine art."

I agreed with Rollo. Darius Pierre, the dealer who runs the gallery, specializes in lifeless sculptures and inoffensive paintings, Muzak for the eyes, that you'd expect to see on the walls of a dentist's waiting room or in the lobby of a three-star hotel.

"Must be worth a fortune," I said.

"Too bad the artist won't see any of it," said Barnes.

I looked for a name on the card beside the sculpture, but I couldn't see anything but the title of the piece: "Madam Butterfly plays the air guitar."

"Who's the artist?" I said.

"For a long time people thought his name was Michel Rondelle," said Barnes.

"Never heard of him," I said.

"You probably won't," said Barnes.

"Why's that?"

"He's dead."

Barnes said he'd tell me more about Michel Rondelle if I had time. "You might like the story," he said.

"It's April," I said. "What else do I have to do?"

Once I heard the details from Rollo, I did some digging. I checked the details in the trial transcripts. I talked to everyone who'd known Michel Rondelle, his brother and the other characters involved in his scheme. I went back through the archives of my own paper and checked other scandal sheets that thrive on feeding readers' insatiable appetite for lurid gossip about the idle rich. And after I waded through all that, I wrote it all down. Here's the story.

PART ONE

"Droll thing life is – that mysterious arrangement
of merciless logic for a futile purpose."
Joseph Conrad

One

If you live in America, you need to shop, even when you go on vacation. If you go on vacation in Palm beach, you go shopping on Worth Avenue.

If you'd been there early one Tuesday morning in October, you would have seen a few early-rising pedestrians promenading along the immaculate sidewalk past shops that had yet to open. Most of the pedestrians wore the uniform of wealth, identifying themselves as members of the tribe to which money entitled them to belong. Tanned, silver-haired men in pressed blue jeans, with pastel sweaters in rich shades of cantaloupe and lilac draped over their shoulders, strolled arm-in-arm with women in white trousers and patterned silk blouses. The men's velvet loafers looked as if they seldom touched pavement. A couple of women in yoga pants and dazzling white running shoes hurried past, holding fifty-dollar refillable coffee mugs in their manicured fingers. Like the town of Palm Beach, all of them looked well ordered, prosperous, meticulously clean and polished to a rich sheen, complementing their surroundings like models in a catalogue. But on this particular morning you would also have noticed a couple of outsiders, a man and a woman who looked as out of place on Worth Avenue as two pimples on the cheek of a super model. The woman wore tattered jean shorts over a torn purple leotard with a pair of black Doc Martins on her feet. Her hair was purple, and she wore a gold stud in her nose. The man was dressed from head to foot in black and was carrying a plastic shopping bag from Piggly Wiggly. While the other pedestrians walked with studied nonchalance on their pilgrimage past the country's most exclusive retail shops, these two stopped frequently to stare with undisguised and embarrassing lust not just at displays of watches, clothing, carpets and bric-a-brac in the shop windows but also at the cars parked by the curb, which included a Bentley, a Bugatti and an Aston Martin. If you'd been more curious and less-self-conscious than the other pedestrians on the street that morning, you might have looked more closely at this couple and seen that the woman, beneath her punk-rocker veneer, was actually an adolescent girl trying hard and succeeding from a distance to present herself as a worldly adult. As for her companion, he'd emerged from an adolescent world of fear, hostility and aggression with a hardness that would have intimidated a rattlesnake.

Outside a jewellery shop called Kaufmann de Suisse, the girl stopped to admire a collection of bracelets in the window. One of them in particular caught her eye, rubies mounted in gold, surrounded by sapphires.

"Like it?" said the man

"Sure," said the girl.

The man held up the plastic bag. "We sell these? I'm gonna buy it for you, baby."

The girl squeezed his arm and drew him closer.

Through the window, the man noticed a saleswoman arranging necklaces on a display counter. He went to the door and pulled the handle, but the door was locked. The woman inside noticed him, though, and came to the entrance. At first, she looked eager to invite him into the shop. No one seeks entry to a jewellery store at nine o'clock in the morning unless he wants to buy something. But when she looked at the man more closely, the expression on her face changed, as if she'd walked to her car and found one of the tires had gone flat. She shook her head and mouthed the words, "We're closed."

"I just wondered about that bracelet in the window," the man said.

The clerk shook her head again and held her hand to her ear. The man spoke more loudly. His words echoed through the deserted street like a handful of gravel tossed into an empty cathedral. The clerk looked at him for a moment, shrugged and turned away.

For a moment, the man looked as if he might punch his fist through the glass, but he changed his mind.

"Bitch," he muttered.

He and the girl stopped at the shop next door to look at three identical mannequins dressed in identical purple ball gowns. As they stood there, a woman in a yellow pantsuit stopped at the door of the jewellery shop and pushed a buzzer. A moment later, they heard the lock open, and the woman walked inside.

"I'll be back," the man muttered to himself.

He and the girl walked farther along the sidewalk and turned into a mews, walked past two or three small storefronts and an Italian restaurant called Bice and stopped outside the M2 Gallery. The door was unlocked. Inside, they found the owner seated at a table near the back of the gallery. He was wearing sunglasses, but he took them off when he saw the man walking toward him. He smiled and rose to his feet. He was wearing a pink sports jacket over a red T-shirt. He wasn't tall. Behind the table, he was visible only above his crotch.

"Mary Louise," he nodded at the girl. "Right on time."

He looked at the man in black and held out his hand. "Darius Pierre," he said.

The man introduced himself as Mike Rondell.

Mike set the shopping bag on the table and pulled out three wooden carvings of lizards. He tilted his head toward Mary Louise. "She says you might be interested in this."

Darius pushed aside a stack of catalogues so that he could look more closely at one of the carvings. When he did, he held his breath the same way as I did a few years later. He examined the sculpture for almost a minute without saying a word. Then he nodded his head. "Incredible," he said. "Where did you get it?"

"It's mine," said Mike.

"You made it?" said Darius.

"That's what I said."

Darius looked at Mary Louise. "We saw something like this at a flea market," he said.

"My brother," said Mike. "He sells them for me. He knows fuck all about art."

Darius held up another carving. He started babbling about "the barely repressed aggression", "the rough edges", "the flow." He talked about depth and technique. He turned the sculpture over to look at it more closely. He talked about tone and force. He said the piece was assertive yet sensitive. "Attractive qualities in a work of art," Darius said. He looked at Mary Louise. "Or a woman."

"You're high," said Mary Louise. Darius watched her drift away to look at a framed print on the gallery wall.

"That's a Rollo Barnes," he said.

"I told Mike about him," said Mary Louise.

"The one beside it is a Kit White," said Darius.

"I don't know him," said Mary Louise.

Darius returned his attention to the sculpture in his hands. He spoke in rapid bursts. Some artists master the tools and conventions of their craft, he said, without capturing an audience for their work. They may be ahead of their time, but they give our lives continuity and beauty. You can trace your cultural lineage through Shakespeare to the Greeks, even further, to the Indo-European origins of art and language. "But then you have a shark in a Plexiglas tank," he said. "Or a pile of stones in the corner of a room. Where's the convention in that? What artistic tools did it require to get the fish into the box? And why is that particular fish in that particular box worth millions, when any other fish in any other box would be worth less than nothing?"

"No idea," said Mike.

"Perhaps the artist wants to draw our attention to the art that exists all around us."

"Could be," said Mike.

"Then there's provenance," said Darius.

"Rhode Island," said Mike.

Darius laughed. He talked about adding Mike's sculptures to the Kleppman and Merriwether collections, which already included post-modern works, he said, by artists Mike had never heard of.

"How much will they pay?" said Mike.

"How much do you want?" Darius said.

Mike thought for a moment. "Two, three hundred."

He waited for Darius to laugh. He couldn't believe he was asking for so much money. But he'd conducted enough drug deals to know that he had to start high and work his way down before he reached a price that would satisfy both of them. He looked directly into Darius's eyes and dared the little ponce to challenge him.

Darius shook his head. "I can't sell them at that price," he said.

"One-fifty, then. Two hundred for the big one."

"You don't understand," said Darius.

Mike became agitated. "I can't go lower," Mike said.

"Not lower," said Darius. "Higher."

"How much?" Mike said.

"Add some zeroes," Darius said.

"Fifteen hundred," Mike said.

Darius shook his head again. Mike thought he might have misheard him. There were already two zeroes in the number.

"Thousand?" Mike said.

"Make it twenty," Darius said. "Anything lower, no one will look at it."

"You're shitting me," Mike said.

"You think that's expensive?" Darius said. "People in Palm Beach pay eight hundred thousand dollars to keep their grass cut. You know what Nelson Pelz pays in property taxes? One point eight million. Why would they buy a piece of art that a high-school principal can afford? They expect to pay more. They want to pay more. Would you like to do a couple of lines?"

Darius poured a mound of cocaine on the surface of the table, squared it with an X-acto knife into lines and handed Mike a rolled-up hundred-dollar bill. Mike moved around the table and stood beside Darius. He inhaled the coke. Mary Louise returned to the table and did a line, too.

"Besides," said Darius, "if we price it right, my client can use it as a tax write-off."

Mary Louise wandered away again toward the front of the gallery.

As the coke kicked in, Mike stared at Darius, getting high and watching the man's lips move while he talked. The thought of twenty thousand dollars excited him. He could buy himself a car. He could buy new clothes and go to bars in Palm Beach to meet rich women. He could go back to the jewellery store on Worth Avenue and wave a few thousand-dollar bills in the face of the cow behind the door until she opened up and sold him the bracelet in the window.

"What are you thinking?" Darius said.

"A chick in a jewellery store," Mike said. "Down the street."

Darius ran his fingers along the side of the wooden lizard. His hands were slender. His fingernails were manicured. "Jewels would be a nice touch," he said.

He reached under the table and handed Mike a clear plastic tube. "Emeralds and rubies," Darius said. "My clients love sparklers."

"Rubies?" Mike said.

"And emeralds," said Darius. "Just chips. They're not worth much."

"You want these on the sculptures," Mike said.

"A pavé. Along one flank," Darius said. He reached out and laid his fingertips against Mike's waist. Mike didn't flinch.

"I have to get to school," said Mary Louise returning from the front of the gallery. "Mind if I take this?" She held up an art magazine that she'd picked up from the table.

Darius shrugged. "Take it," he said. "They're free."

He picked up a sculpture.

"We'll need more like this," he said.

"When do you need them?" said Mike.

"Soon."

"Sure," Mike said.

"And then we'll introduce you to Palm Beach."

"I can't wait," Mike said.

Outside the gallery, Mike handed the bag and the tube of gemstone chips to Mary Louise.

"What am I supposed to do with these?" she said.

"Give 'em to Dwayne. Tell him we need a pavé. Along one flank. Like this." He put his hand on her waist and ran it over her hip to rest on her butt. "He'll know what to do."

They walked two blocks to Chilean Avenue and got into a Datsun pickup parked by the curb. It took fifteen minutes to cross the bridge to West Palm Beach and drive to Mary Louise's high school. By the time they got there, Darius Pierre had gone to work on his newest artist.

Two

It took a few weeks, but it seemed to happen almost overnight. From a rough-edged, small-town Canadian tough guy, Darius Pierre transformed Mike Rondel into a celebrated sculptor with a Gallic pedigree. He prepared a potted biography of the artist. He included a list of the galleries where Michel Rondelle had shown his work, the museums that had acquired at least one of his sculptures and the corporations whose collections included one of his pieces. He arranged with a friend to produce documents that verified the provenance of Rondelle's sculptures, with references to the Kleppman and Merriwether collections. With the biography, catalogue and documentation of the rising sale prices, Darius persuaded an influential critic from the New York art world to write a flattering, semi-literate article about Michel Rondelle in a magazine called *Art Internationale*. Six times a year, twenty thousand collectors and art enthusiasts on the magazine's mailing list received a free copy, which they could display prominently in their homes to impress their visitors. The magazine carried advertisements for Hennessy cognac, Patek Philippe watches and Heesen yachts and charged a fee to artists and their agents to place positive reviews in its pages. Most of its readers assumed that the art displayed within its covers was as desirable as the products in the advertisements. Directed by Darius Pierre, Michel Rondelle emerged that year onto the Palm Beach art scene like a comet in the night sky. To many of us, his arrival seemed as sudden, unexpected and, ultimately, tragic as the death of a child in a car wreck.

While he waited for Mike to deliver more sculptures, Darius shepherded the first ones, each with a certificate of authenticity signed by the artist and stamped with the artist's initials under its neck, through the hands of five buyers before he offered them to carefully selected collectors in Palm Beach. These collectors had to be rich enough to afford the work, but not so established as connoisseurs that they could ignore his promise of embellishing their reputations. All of them aspired to a higher echelon in Palm Beach society, and they felt frustrated by the obstacles of taste, character and pedigree that stood in their way. They might have bought a membership in Mar-a-Lago for two hundred thousand dollars, but no one would invite them to join the Everglades Club. A reputation as a connoisseur of fine art might help them to overcome these obstacles. They also had to be jealous enough of the other collectors that, if one of them bought a sculpture by Michel Rondelle, the others wouldn't dismiss the artist as a talentless, over-hyped charlatan; they'd find a way to buy one of Rondelle's pieces for themselves.

Knowing that an artist's work becomes more desirable to one client if another client wants the same piece, Darius offered one of the lizards for fifty thousand dollars to Estaban Morales, the former finance minister of Venezuela, who had embezzled three billion dollars from his country's treasury and now kept a stable of thoroughbred horses in Wellington. Then Darius told Hamilton Roebuck, the grocery magnate, that he had only one of Michel Rondelle's sculptures left to sell. Neither man knew anything about art nor could he persuade his wife to allow the piece in their home, so they took Darius's advice and sold their pieces to a third collector, at a higher price, and each of them made money on the deal. The third collector then sold one of his lizards to a dealer in New York who had been associated with Larry Salander, the fraudulent dealer who was serving time in prison on Rikers Island, and had worked in the past with Darius on similar transactions. The other lizard remained in Palm Beach, where Darius sold it to Leonard Friesen, the chemical weapons dealer, reassuring him that Keith Kleppman, a wealthy investment dealer, wanted to buy a Rondelle sculpture, as well. Friesen idolized Keith Kleppman and flattered him with excessive imitation, right down to his red suspenders and his Cuban cigars. By the time Friesen bought his piece, the price had risen by more than one hundred eighty per cent. That was the price that Keith Kleppman paid for his Rondelle sculpture, although he intended to sell it and double his money as soon as Darius had stirred the embers of desire for such rare and precious works of art.

As art-world hustles go, none of these transactions drew much attention. They didn't change the minds of people who thought of Darius Pierre as a shallow and superficial man who thought the world would regard him as an extraordinary person if he looked as if he was. Deeply tanned, he resembled an aging surfer who hadn't come to terms with the passing of time. He dressed like a parrot in rainbow-hued designer clothes and never appeared in public without a silk scarf wrapped loosely around his neck. He dropped names into his conversations like a trout fisherman dropping flies into a fast-moving river. The frames of his glasses were mauve, and he had ten pairs. I've never trusted tanned men who wear sunglasses indoors and look like beach bums. But as I got to know him better I discovered, under his flamboyant façade, a complexity of ambition, fear, desire, paranoia, entitlement, intelligence, sensitivity and ambiguity and a raw and vulnerable spirit that he guarded from other people even as he kept it open and receptive to the dynamic forces of art. I've seen him respond with manic enthusiasm to the paintings of Joan Mitchell. Listening to a Beethoven string quartet that he'd heard a dozen times, he still weeps quietly. But of all the passions that drive Darius Pierre, the one that prevails is greed.

In Palm Beach, Darius acquired a reputation for identifying emerging artists whose work rose in price as they became better known. He did this like a stock broker tipping an investor to an undervalued security. Sometimes a client or a dealer invited him to bring a piece to his home, where Darius would spend the night drinking, snorting coke and sleeping with the man or woman, if that's what it took to make a sale. At other times, he kept his clients' artwork in storage while its prices appreciated until they could sell it again at a handsome profit.

Most of the men on Darius's client list regard art in the same way as they regard macramé or roller skating. They think they have more important things to do than choose a painting that matches the carpet in the dining room, so they give their wives a budget and leave it to them to put suitable paintings on the wall and sculptures in the nooks and alcoves of their homes. A few of the women have studied fine art at college and know the difference between a Monet and a Manet, but most of them work with interior decorators to advise them on the latest trends in the art world. Darius cultivated his relationships with decorators in Palm Beach like Mimsi Macklin, Patsy Palladoni and Piper Shanahan-Morgan, all of whom turn to him when they need a piece of art that will draw attention to their clients' good taste without offending anyone's sensibilities.

In return for the thousand small, complex tasks that Darius performs to help his clients build their collections, they pay him a handsome fee. Storage, shipping, condition reports, restoration, making copies, framing, due diligence, insurance: for all these services, he charges an extra two per cent of the purchase price of any work he sells.

Darius offers his clients an opportunity to reduce their taxes, as well. As a prominent auctioneer once told me, art is transportable, unregulated, glamorous, arcane, beautiful and difficult. It's easier to store than oil, more esoteric than diamonds, more durable than political influence. And its elusive valuation makes it conducive to extremely creative tax accounting. In Europe, Darius can sell artwork for a couple of thousand euros to straw men, who receive a cut when they resell the same piece for ten or twenty times that amount. In this way he not only makes a handsome profit, but also avoids paying commission to the artist and taxes on the resale. For clients who become embroiled in lawsuits involving their art transactions, Darius maintains a satellite office in Liechtenstein, where it's against the law to investigate a business if the matter is related to an offshore criminal lawsuit. Few of his clients have ever lost a lawsuit.

This makes Darius Pierre a popular figure in Palm Beach, where A-type personalities compete to win at all costs, whether they're negotiating to take over an oil company or playing cribbage with their wives. These men may have no strong attraction to the art that they buy, but they have an insatiable drive to beat anyone who threatens their sense of superiority, whether it's based on art, houses, investments, cars or women.

To win his clients' confidence, Darius manages an artist in the same way as Procter & Gamble manages Tide laundry detergent, as a brand. He knows that any commercial artist with a lithograph machine could create a painting comparable to Andy Warhol's unidimensional monoprints, but only Warhol had the drive to sacrifice his humanity, with all its rough edges, conundrums, joys, contradictions and second guesses, to turn himself into a sleek desirable brand with the mass appeal of an O Henry chocolate bar. A Warhol appeals to collectors, Darius told me, in the same way as an Armani handbag or Lamborghini sports car. Backed by a ruthless and well-run corporate machine, these brands hold their value as they age or, in Warhol's case, after they die.

Managed as a brand, an artist can generate sustainable value as long as the brand informs everything he does, from the way he dresses and cuts his hair to where he lives, what he eats for dinner and who eats it with him. Without wasting time on research or contemplation, a client can look at an artist like Warhol, Jeff Koons or Michel Rondelle and know exactly what the brand stands for. In the art world of Darius Pierre, the label counts for much more than the content. By the time Mike called Darius and invited him to pick up more sculptures at an address on North K Street, in Lake Worth, the brand called Michel Rondelle had been launched. Only the man himself needed attention from Darius.

Darius drove that afternoon across the drawbridge to Lake Worth. When he turned up North K Street, he felt as if he'd entered another universe. He was less than two miles from Palm Beach, where he'd stayed every year for fifteen years with a widow named Melanie Merriwether, but in all those years he'd never ventured into this neighborhood. The houses seemed flimsy and temporary. Some had small, well-tended gardens and looked trim and ordered, but they all gave off the same scent of desperation and imperma-nence as his childhood home in Erie. A stiff breeze, a heavy rain, a bolt of lightning, a falling tree could rip the houses apart and scatter their residents hither and yon like sneeze-blown grains of pepper over a tabletop. Front yards were littered with the artifacts of American life – washing machines, old computers, a toilet, a TV, a bathtub, a box spring, aluminum windows, an office chair, a plastic EXIT sign from a grocery store, blue plastic pop cases filled with broken hand tools and empty detergent bottles, and, in almost every driveway, a car on cinder blocks – all discarded like yesterday's desires. People in these places squeezed every last penny of value out of stuff be-fore they threw it in the garbage. They furnished their houses with rusted kitchen chairs, wooden cable spools discarded by the power company and sprung chesterfields from evicted relatives and abandoned motels. To cook outdoors, they ran extension cords from plugs inserted into their porch lights to electric frying pans on TV dinner tables, where they fried their evening meal of chipped beef and sliced potatoes. People here might try to pull themselves up by their bootstraps, but they clung to subsistence by their fingernails. They knew that one lapse in judgment, one bad hangover, one arrest for a traffic violation that kept them from their job at WalMart or the lumber yard, one miscalculated outburst of anger would send them over the brink. A few of them clawed their way out. But most of them lost their grip, descended into poverty and then started over, from scratch. But for all their inelegance and tasteless clutter, he felt a sense of comfort here that he'd felt as a child but never felt in Palm Beach.

When he found the address that Mike had given him, he parked in the driveway and walked to the front door, where Mike met him with the three sculptures. He didn't invite him inside. Darius took the sculptures from Mike and started to walk back to the car.

"Hold on," said Mike. "I'll go with you."

At the gallery, Darius engraved the stylized initials MR in the wood under the creatures' necks "to confirm their authenticity," he said.

Looking at the jeweled sculptures, he said it was time now to introduce Michel Rondelle to his patron, Melanie Merriwether. Her endorsement would position Rondelle firmly within the cold and heartless embrace of the moneyed Palm Beach art world. Then he gave Mike nine thousand dollars in cash. Mike used the money to buy a used Dodge Challenger 440 Magnum GT, whose mileage was equivalent to fifty round-trips across the United States. With another thousand dollars, he put a deposit on a one-bedroom apartment in Lantana, near Hypoluxo Road.

Three

Mike remembered pulling up in his Challenger to the gates of the Merriwether property and looking beyond the perimeter hedge at the flower gardens tastefully planted with calla lilies, bougainvillea, gardenias, datura and hibiscus. A velvet-green lawn ran as flat and smooth as a billiard table from the road to the shore of the inland waterway. When the gates opened, he remembered the sound of his tires rolling over the gravel driveway like a wave retreating over a sandy beach.

At the side of the house he stopped under a portico. Within seconds, a Filipino maid opened the door. Mike was dressed in black, but on instructions from Darius, had tied one of Darius's exotic silk scarves around his waist.

"She looked at me like I was a fucking ponce," he told me later.

"You can't park here," she said.

Mike told the maid that he'd come to meet Melanie Merriwether. The maid looked skeptical, until a dark-haired attendant dressed in white emerged from inside the house. "It's all right, Betina," he said. "We're expecting him."

He held the door open for Mike.

"Give me your keys," he said.

Leaving Mike in the doorway, he walked to the car, inserted himself behind the wheel and drove the car around the corner of the house and out of sight. Mike hoped the upholstery wouldn't leave grease stains on the man's white polo shirt.

Mike said later he'd never forget his first glimpse of the interior of Melanie's house: Walls with the rich sheen of vanilla ice cream. Ceilings so high, he'd have needed a ladder to reach them. Two marble staircases descending in symmetrical curves like over-sized earrings from the floor above. Sculptures on polished and spotless tabletops under lighting so discrete, he had to search for its source. Passageways ahead and to both sides offering a choice of directions to walk through the house. Footsteps echoing through doorways that led to rooms beyond rooms like images in a barbershop mirror.

To either side of the door were two matching love seats, one supporting a teddy bear from Hermés and the other, a silk-covered pillow embroidered with the words, "You don't know how many friends you have until you move to Palm Beach." His black pants were clean, but Mike didn't dare to sit down on the white upholstery. On a low table beside each love seat sat an identical over-sized art book in a crimson calfskin slip-case. The house had the presence of a well-trained waiter, unobtrusive but ready to serve. How much money did it take, Mike wondered, to make a house feel as if nobody lived there?

Mike had spent most of his life crowded into his father's house on Oozloffsky Street in a small town in Ontario called Petrolia. In its cramped low-ceilinged rooms, the paint was chipped, the floor tiles were peeling, and the dysfunctional radiators clanked and rattled without giving off much heat. The place always smelled of fried food, stale beer, cigarette smoke and unwashed bodies. The dingy hallway and front porch were cluttered with baby strollers, rubber boots, scooters, paint cans and auto parts stuffed into plastic pop cases. Most of the time, the bare lightbulbs in the ceiling were burnt out or missing. The sounds of barking dogs, loud music and mumbled dialogue from TV sets seeped like aural gas through walls so thin that he could have driven his fist into the next room. Mike shared a room with his half-brother, sleeping on a mattress on the floor. Privacy depended on a cheap hollow door with a fake brass knob that came off in your hand if you turned it too hard. You didn't have to go far to find the bathroom, he said, but you never knew if you'd find soap, toilet paper or a lid on the toilet.

In Melanie's house, there were no stains or scuff marks on the gleaming marble floors, no hand prints or patches of crumbled plaster on the walls, no smells of stale beer or yesterday's dinner. The air smelled as clean as the walls. It smelled like money, and Mike couldn't get enough of it.

He was taking deep breaths and sliding the sole of his loafer back and forth over the polished marble floor when he heard his name and looked up to see Darius descending the stairway to his right. At the bottom of the stairway, Darius paused to examine his reflection in a mirrored panel in the wall. He ran a hand over his blonde hair and adjusted his mauve sweater. Today, he wore no shoes. His bare feet were tanned. He'd spent the morning on his exercise bike, he said, reading an issue of Fortune magazine, which he carried in one hand. When he noticed

Mike looking at the red Kabbalah string around his wrist, Darius said he and Melanie were studying the Torah. He led Mike deeper into the house, glancing into several mirrors as they walked. In Melanie Merriwether's house, you were never far from a mirror.

Through distant doorways, Mike noticed people darting like mice through his peripheral vision: Betina, the maid, flitting across a hallway; a tall butler in a black suit disappearing into a room to his left. Through the windows he noticed teams of gardeners pruning and coddling plants, another man climbing a ladder to the roof of the garage, two men using mesh baskets on long poles to skim random leaves from the still surface of the swimming pool and a third man with a hose.

"Busy around here," said Mike.

"You're never alone in Palm Beach," said Darius. "Lonely, perhaps. But not alone."

Darius could sympathize with Mike's reaction. They had more in common than Mike could ever have imagined. Before he met Melanie, Darius had studied theater arts at a community college in Erie, Pennsylvania. His name then had been Troy Tillman. From the time he was born, his mother thought he resembled a handsome blonde TV actor named Troy Donohue, and she hoped that her son might follow the teenaged heartthrob into the fame and fortune of movie stardom. When he was older, she paid for his college program from her income as an accounting clerk for a sewing-supply company. But when her son remained unknown and undiscovered after two years, she sent him to New York with a check for two hundred dollars and an introduction to a distant cousin, who was an assistant director of marketing at Bloomingdale's. In New York, her son changed his name to Darius Pierre and went to work as an underwear model and window dresser at the store. He'd been there for six months when a co-worker invited him one afternoon to a fashion show at the Park Avenue Armory. Waiting for a champagne cocktail at the crowded bar, he'd impulsively adjusted the scarf around the neck of a short, plump, dark-haired woman beside him. In those days, he did things like that. The woman was Melanie Merriwether. Melanie was feeling adventurous that day, and Darius was feeling heterosexual, and each of them was drunk. Relationships have begun under less auspicious circumstances.

Melanie invited Darius to dinner that night with some friends at Café Boulud. She was in her late thirties, only recently widowed for the second time. Finding herself amused and distracted by Darius, she asked him after dinner to go with her to Europe. Darius thought she was joking. But two days later, Melanie's private secretary contacted him with the tail number of her jet and said a limousine would take him to Teterboro Airport in New Jersey. Darius packed a change of clothes and a toothbrush and never went back to Bloomingdale's. After that, he and Melanie seldom spent a day apart, whether they were in New York, London, Hong Kong or Palm Beach. Almost every day, Melanie reminded him that they were more than business partners, less than lovers and certainly not husband and wife, implicit or otherwise.

Darius adapted easily to his new life. He exercised his gift for conversation, learned when to step forward with a comment and when to step back and listen. He learned to drive an Aston Martin. He learned to give orders to people who were paid to obey him, and he backed up his orders with Melanie's money. He was an accomplished mimic and he knew how to dress according to Melanie's station in life. He could recognize a Givenchy gown, a Patek Philippe watch or a Julian Opie painting without looking at the label. He could dance the tango till dawn with the louche elegance of an Argentinian polo player and, four hours later, accompany Melanie to mass at Saint Edward and kneel before Monsignor Klinzing like a choirboy in a Brooks Brothers suit.

As often happens to people who derive their sense of self-importance from another person's money, Darius became a snob. Numbed, pampered and chronically deluded, he developed the necessary arrogance of an acolyte as he followed Melanie through her day. No one could freeze a presumptuous sales clerk or cut short an uppity waiter with more sangfroid than Darius Pierre. No one could show disdain more pointedly for an ill-dressed fruit-picker on a rusty bicycle impeding his progress in his Aston Martin along the A1A. Darius knew how much to tip a doorman and how to give him the money: folded twice, as if the twenty-dollar bill were a piece of worthless lint from the pocket of his Stefano Ricci jacket. He knew that you never made eye contact unless a person had something that you wanted. In social conversations, he knew how to use as many words as possible to say absolutely nothing and to infuse every syllable with unctuous sincerity.

Some people in Palm Beach regard Darius Pierre as Melanie Merriwether's walker. It isn't exactly an insult. Walkers are a hot commodity in Palm Beach. Through study or breeding they've acquired good manners and a sense of decorum. They dress well. They can conduct a conversation with wit and humor. They know which fork to use at dinner, they chew with their mouths closed, and they can dance. Most important, they're men.

Walkers like Jimmy Galavanos and Ted Montfort live in bachelor apartments in South Palm Beach, spend their evenings at the Colony and accompany rich widows to dinners and dances throughout the Season. They

33

glide through the social scene like eagles on a thermal, but occasionally, like Jimmy Galavanos, they get their feathers ruffled. One night Jimmy drove to West Palm in his red Ferarri with Francine Delmont, the widow of a Caterpillar heavy equipment dealer, and found a taxi parked in the spot that he regarded as his own, in front of Bradley's Saloon. When the cabbie refused to move, Jimmy pulled a gun from a crotch holster and threatened to shoot him. The confrontation angered the cab driver and embarrassed Francine Delmont, but it might never have happened if she'd treated Jimmy the way Melanie Merriwether treated Darius Pierre.

For one thing, she allowed him to live on her property. In return for his presence as her companion, amusement, distraction, sexual dalliance, dance partner, art advisor and gallery manager, Melanie gave Darius a two-bedroom apartment above her garage and a salary of three hundred thousand dollars a year.

During the season Darius had free access to one of Melanie's two Aston Martins, which he used to take clients to dinner, on Melanie's tab, at a restaurant near the gallery called Bice. She paid for his thrice-weekly visits to a psychiatrist and the prescription drugs he took to keep his depression in check while he did his best to convince himself that he found her seductively attractive. So far, this arrangement had lasted for fifteen years.

Leading Mike through the house, Darius remembered the days after he'd first come here with Melanie Merriwether. Trying to relax by the pool, he, too, had felt self-conscious in the presence of so many people. All day long, there was someone within ten feet of him: a gardener, maid, pool boy, nanny, cleaning lady, painter, carpenter, handyman, chef, personal trainer, florist, therapist. They burst out of hedges, popped out of closets, invaded quiet rooms with vacuum cleaners and drove lawn mowers past windows that overlooked the gardens. Noisy, furtive, submissive, assertive, they were always in motion, even when they had nothing to do. To each other, they spoke Spanish, Tagalog, Urdu or Russian. When they spoke in English to Darius or Melanie, they did it with an accent, conveying information with deferential humor about a worn carpet or a dying rose bush that needed attention, usually at great expense. Face to face with Darius, they were preternaturally polite. They might want to stab him in the back with a paring knife or run over him with the golf cart they used to ferry the trash barrels to the shed behind the pool house, but he would never know it, because they would never admit it. Even when they looked him in the eye, he never knew what they were really thinking. Transparency doesn't keep you employed for long in Palm Beach. Eventually Darius had become accustomed to their presence in the same way as he'd become accustomed to the tree outside the music room and the view of Lake Worth from the bedroom window. They were part of the landscape.

Melanie and her friends in Palm Beach paid these people to do what most people do for themselves: unpack a suitcase, make a bed, change a lightbulb, adjust the TV, pay a bill, wash the dishes, wash the car, walk the dog, write a thank-you note, select a birthday gift. They paid doctors to evaluate their health and psychiatrists to rid them of inconvenient emotions like anger, shame, despair and envy that sullied their enjoyment of their good fortune like a bruise on an apple.

Since Darius had insinuated himself into her life, Melanie had cut back on her therapy sessions to three days a week. Now she relied on Darius for the comfort she'd obtained from talking about herself for hours on end. In many ways, Darius had more to offer Melanie than a conventional therapist. He was certainly better looking, and as her live-in companion, he was available at any time of the day or night.

In the music room, Melanie sat at one of two matching Bosendorfer pianos. "She said she'd come from the gym, but I knew just from looking at her that she was rich," said Mike. "Something about her skin, maybe, her face or her hair. In layers, like, with gold flecks. Highlights. She wasn't that good-looking. Kind of chunky. A bit overweight. But you could tell she spent a lot of time making herself look good."

If he'd looked more closely, he'd have noticed that Melanie paid a lot of money to look casual. She was wearing Dolce & Gabbana yoga pants and a black T-shirt, for which she'd paid almost two thousand dollars. On her feet she wore a pair of canvas espadrilles from Kiki D's on Worth Avenue that had been dyed in a seaside shanty near Dover, England, in a vat filled with liquefied petals from thirty thousand gentian flowers hand-picked by small boys from the local priory. Melanie had paid two thousand dollars for the shoes, of which the school received an eleven-dollar donation to its orienteering program. All of this information enhanced the comfort and pride she took from wearing these shoes and justified their price.

Melanie had just finished a session with her personal trainer, a Swede named Ulf, who had arrived that morning from New York. She brought Ulf to Palm Beach on her personal jet for five days every month. This morning he'd led her through a series of exercises in the gym downstairs that involved raising and lowering her arms and balancing on one foot. The exercises were so easy, a child could have done them, but Melanie liked to brag about the demands imposed by Ulf on her strength and endurance. After he left, she stopped doing the exercises until he returned. She simply couldn't stay motivated, she told her friends, without Ulf. If she had to motivate herself to exercise, she worried that she'd gain weight.

It was late morning, the best time of day for Melanie. The prescription drugs were taking effect, and she hadn't had her first cocktail. It was the time of day, she said, when she felt herself standing on top of the world, looking down on creation. She hadn't gone out of her way for the occasion of her first meeting with Mike. He was just an artist, after all. Self-proclaimed artists are a dime a dozen in Palm Beach. On her way to the music room, she'd talked for a moment to the head gardener, whose staff of cousins and half-brothers from Honduras kept the grounds in impeccable condition, and told him about the leaves cluttering the grass beside the reflecting pool.

Now, as Darius led Mike into the room, she said, "You're another one of Darius's discoveries." She smiled by moving nothing but her lips. "How nice. For you."

Melanie had met several artists whose work Darius carried in the M2 Gallery. Their pieces reminded her of a high-fashion handbag or a Paloma Picasso bracelet: shiny, expensive but not too challenging. Most of the artists were gay, which appealed to her sense of symmetry and order. Two men in a gay relationship never had to deal with disturbing heterosexual ambiguities. Even their parts matched. They presented themselves as swashbucklers of the soul, dashing and impulsive men who had little regard for convention or propriety. They followed their hearts, guided only by passion and regarded with disdain more conventional men of reason, like her former husband, whose sole purpose in life was making money. And they dressed so well and kow-towed in such an amusing way to anyone wealthy enough to buy their stuff. But Darius had warned her that this artist was different. How had he put it? "A semi-literate tattooed ex-hockey player from some Canadian hick town like Moose Jaw." Still, Melanie expected to meet another sycophantic mediocrity in a pastel sweater and madras trousers, honking about the bad taste of his Republican clients.

To her surprise, this one really was different. Dressed in well-pressed but shabby black pants and a tight black shirt, a mauve scarf tossed casually around his neck, he had slick black hair and chiseled features. Through his shirt she sensed a well-muscled body and she felt herself drawn to the obsidian hardness of his blue eyes. He looked vaguely foreign and reminded her of her father. She sensed the same toughness, the same potential for viciousness, the same hard heart. She preferred softer men, but she didn't understand them, and they eventually bored her. Even though she felt anxious around tough men, they also excited her, the way Mike did now. Men who treated her with courtesy and respect aroused her suspicions. She figured they wanted something from her. Every time she became involved with a nice man, she ended up trying to humiliate him.

"You speak English?" she said.

Mike studied her face, suspecting that she was joking. "Yes," he said. Then, remembering his embellished identity, he added, "Un peu."

Melanie turned her attention to the three lizards that Darius had positioned on the closed lid of the piano. Against the polished mahogany, under the soft light, the creatures looked as if they were breathing. She could hardly take her eyes off them.

"These are yours," she said to Mike. She stood up to take a closer look.

"That's right," Mike said.

He watched Melanie as she stared at the figures.

"I don't like the jewels," she said.

Mike looked at Darius. "You told me she wanted jewels."

"Darius knows I don't like jewels," Melanie said.

"I have others," said Mike. "Without jewels."

"I'd like to see them," she said.

"These aren't for you," said Darius. "These are for Kleppman."

"Do you like parties, Miguel?" said Melanie.

"Michel," said Darius.

Melanie said, "We'll arrange an evening. Introduce you to our local art world. I suppose we'll have to invite Kleppman. You'll have to introduce him, Darius."

Now she glanced at Mike. "Nice to meet you, Mark," she said. She stood up then and walked out of the room.

"Good," Darius said. "She likes your work."

"Better tell her my name's Mike. Or Michel."

"She doesn't remember names."

"And Kleppman?"

"What about him?"

"She remembers his name."

"He's our neighbor," said Darius.

"Mary Louise told me about his parties."

"Let's go back to my place," said Darius.

He reached around Mike's waist and pulled him closer. "We can talk about it there."

Mike said he would have decked the little prick, but he wanted more money and, no matter what he had to do, he intended to get it.

Four

People in Palm Beach accept each other at face value, the way you do when you're on vacation and you've put your critical faculties to rest. If you say you're rich and look as if you are, they'll take your word for it, and they won't ask you how you made your money. But I work here. It's my job to look beyond appearances. Behind the bland façade of money, there's always a more interesting story.

Money enabled Melanie Merriwether to indulge her eccentricities, but it never helped her to feel safe. She worried constantly about running out of it, and she suspected that everyone she met would try to steal it from her. Her paranoia left her marooned on an island of wealth and removed her from the great ocean of humanity. She derived more pleasure from her garden than she did from other people, and she regarded her plants as part of her extended family. Every year, she spent five weeks in Italy, at an ecological retreat near Torviscosa, where she meditated, fasted and recorded the melodies of orchids. During this period, she adopted the name Felix Hibiscus, in keeping with the custom of the eco-village of naming individuals after an animal and a plant. In Palm Beach, she positioned miniature speakers throughout the grounds of her house over which she played to other plants the recorded songs of the orchids. Sometimes she would lie beside her plumbago plants with her eyes closed, sensing their bio-emissions. Melanie treated her garden as her surrogate family.

Today she was sitting in the garden with her event planner, an enthusiastic bon vivant named Benoit, discussing the party where she would introduce Michel Rondelle to the Palm Beach art world, raise money for charity by selling some of his sculptures at auction and swindle her neighbors into paying even higher prices for the sculptures than Darius had received from his initial sales. Benoit was well known in Palm Beach for his flamboyance and attention to detail. He'd organized the wedding reception in Monaco for Pierre Casiraghi and Beatrice Borromeo, daughter of the Count of Arona, and the twenty-fifth anniversary party for Steve Cohen, the hedge-fund manager, on the island of Nevis. He was also a shameless gossip. When Melanie told him that the party should remind her guests, in its extravagance, of Gregory Potemkin and Catherine the Great, he said, "I know Potemkin. He's that Russian who bought Trump's house. Made his fortune in peat moss or fertilizer, something dirty and, you know . . ." He waved a manicured hand over his head. "Russian."

Melanie told Benoit that she wanted champagne fountains in the garden "and that sommelier, from Paris. Monsieur What's His Name." She would have included a fireworks exhibition, but a Palm Beach ordnance forbade air bombs and other loud demonstrations. Benoit suggested eight close-up magicians instead.

Melanie wanted elephants, too, but Benoit, knowing his client's pathological aversion to dirt and disorder, reminded her that elephants would eat the flowers and soil the lawn, "the way they did at Doris Duke's masquerade party in Newport," he said. "You can't trust an elephant with a full stomach."

Melanie capitulated on the elephants, but she refused to budge on the dwarfs. "They like to be called little people, dear," said Benoit. By now, Melanie was growing impatient and irritable. "I don't care what you call them," she said. "Just get the little fuckers here."

As an alternative to elephants, Benoit recommended exotic fish in eight gigantic aquariums under soft lighting. "Fish won't drop turds on your lawn," he said. "Your guests can feed them. And they do tricks. Arowana jump right out of the water for a snack."

On his iPad, Benoit found photographs of arowana, flowerhorns and a few other exotic specimens. When Melanie saw one called an axolotl, she noticed that it was, in fact, a salamander, and her eyes lit up.

"Not fish," she said. "Reptiles. We need to find one that's endangered. People love to give money to save an endangered species."

"How about Ebner's skink?" said Benoit. "Elton had one before he got the cocker spaniel."

"Can't we find one with a better name?" said Melanie. "No one spends money to save a skink."

Benoit checked his iPad. "How about the Fijian crested iguana?"

Melanie nodded. "There's our theme," she said. "Night of the Iguana."

"Richard Burton. Elizabeth Taylor," said Benoit. "It's brilliant."

"And Michel's sculptures look like iguanas," said Melanie.

In addition to saving an endangered reptile, Melanie arranged to donate a portion of the auction proceeds to the Institute for Global Sustainability, a think tank based in Washington that generated position papers for Democratic politicians on reducing the reliance by western nations on fossil fuels. She gained clearance from the White House for Al Gore to stop in his private jet at Palm Beach Airport on his way home from a conference on world poverty in Botswana. Because he'd been a vice-president, Melanie received clearance to transport him to her property in a Bell Jet Ranger helicopter, a brief detour in Gore's busy schedule that would consume only five hundred gallons of jet fuel.

Melanie wanted Billy Joel to sing throughout dinner, but she hadn't decided yet on entertainment afterward. Through one of her lawyers, she'd approached Bob Dylan. She said she was prepared to pay any amount of money. One of her neighbors had paid Justin Bieber more than a million dollars to sing two songs at his son's birthday party. Melanie said she'd top that fee, and Dylan would have to play only one song as long as she could choose it. So far, the performer had ignored her invitation. For a million dollars, she knew she could have hired Sting or Kiss or Miley Cyrus, someone who appreciated the value of a dollar. But she wanted Dylan, and she hadn't given up trying.

This gave Benoit another chance to tell his story about John and Yoko in the lobby at the Dakota, when John said he'd have given anything to get the Beatles back together again. "But now that he's gone, I suppose that will never happen," Benoit said, "unless he can bring himself back from the dead. I can always call Mick, I suppose. The Stones will do anything if the money's right. Or maybe Phil can help. Honey, do you remember when you were planning your fiftieth, and Phil called to say he'd send the Ronnettes and the Crystals to sing Happy Birthday?" He pointed across the table at Melanie. "And you told Phil 'Either you send the Righteous Brothers, darling, or don't send anyone at all'." Benoit chuckled at the memory. "Of course, now that he's in jail," he said, "we'd be lucky to get the bloody Teddy Bears."

Eventually, Melanie settled for Vic Damone and Celine Dion. But when Vic Damone died, she agreed reluctantly that Barry Manilow should take his place.

In the days before the party, Melanie's house manager, Paul, instructed the kitchen staff to prepare the best linen, china and silverware. Paul had been the maître d' at the United Nations senior delegates' private dining room in Manhattan. He was accustomed to dealing with self-serving blowhards who lived on other people's money while taking credit for accomplishments of no consequence. He was looking forward to seeing Al Gore again.

For a hundred and twenty-five thousand dollars, Benoit's florist would import a planeload of calla lilies from Amsterdam. Melanie would bring her hairdresser on the jet to Palm Beach from New York to weave pearls on strands of gold thread through her hair. As an afterthought, she decided to place bowls of pearls beside each guest's dessert plate.

Now Melanie got to work on the guest list.

When word got out that she planned to hold another party along with a silent auction to support the Global Sustainability Institute and boost the career of the artist Michel Rondelle, everyone in town hoped to get an invitation. Melanie didn't often open her house to guests. At her last dinner party, to raise funds to preserve an endangered species of leopard, Cyril Gudgeon, the hedge-fund manager, had reached through the bars of a cage and nearly lost an arm. Perhaps this time she'd include another man-eating creature.

Melanie didn't invite the Fanjuls, of course. Popsy Fanjul had once said she'd never be hungry enough to dine under the same roof as Melanie Merriwether, and Melanie didn't want to risk being snubbed by a rich Cuban. She considered inviting Norman Braman, the auto-industry magnate who helped, with his wife, Irma, to set up Art Basel in Miami Beach, but their art collection was much bigger than hers, and she didn't want to embarrass herself. She focused instead on the lower-hanging Palm Beach fruits who could perhaps climb higher up the social tree by accepting her invitation.

The Hornbeams from Detroit, for example, had blundered into Palm Beach when Oscar's third wife, Suzy, a former airline attendant, read about Mar-a-Lago in a travel magazine, heard from her hair dresser that the fortune behind the place had come from sales of Post Rice Krispies made in Michigan and figured that she and Oscar, with their own Michigan pedigree, had something in common with the current occupant. Now Suzy boasted about keeping her perfume in a refrigerator in the bathroom and displaying a hundred Hermes handbags in a glass-doored closet in her bedroom so she could look at them every morning as she dressed herself. Oscar, who was the self-made owner of a national chain of replacement-muffler garages, would never have come to Palm Beach without Suzy's encouragement, and he wasn't especially happy to spend five million dollars on a house on Pelican Lane that didn't offer a view of the ocean. But once they arrived here, he followed her social agenda, whether he liked it or not. Suzy had never heard of Michel Rondelle, but she liked iguanas and she was looking forward to the party so she could get a closer look at some of Melanie's more valuable pieces. "I heard she's trying to sell the Brancusi," she said. "He's very famous." If they bought it, Oscar figured they could put it near the pool house, beside the hot tub.

Melanie included Doctor Cyrus Beltran and his wife, Svetlana, on the invitation list, as well. The Beltrans had been coming to Palm Beach for ten years, ever since Cyrus surprised Svetlana with a thirteen-million-dollar estate on Banyan Road, which they now called "The Birthday Cake." Svetlana once told a reporter from *Vanity Fair* that she prided herself on never wearing the same pair of shoes twice, and she took great delight in describing her annual visits to Harry Winston's, the Manhattan jewelers, where she dug through piles of emeralds and diamonds like a Korean grocer sizing up eggplants. Every year at Christmas, Cyrus wrapped the two brass elephants that flanked the gates in front of the house in gold wrapping paper and red ribbons.

"Such a character," Melanie said. "And the Panama hat. He never takes it off."

With careful calculation and her husband's money, Svetlana Beltran had insinuated herself into the fabric of Palm Beach society, finagling her way into The Society of the Four Arts, the Preservation Foundation and the Flagler Museum. She was involved with the Civic Association, the Community Foundation and the Community Chest United Way. She was on the board of the Belles of St. Mary's Ball, and she supported the Patrons of the Arts in the Vatican Museum. She'd joined the Red Feather Society and the Alexis de Tocqueville Society. All these causes held her aloft like the gases in a hot-air balloon, from where she could look down on the little people without ever having to engage with them in their grubby lives of hopeless struggle unless it furthered her own ambitions. Of course, anyone with the price of a ticket can go to the Palm Beach Day Academy Golf Tournament or the Food for the Poor's Annual Fine Wines & Hidden Treasure Gala at Mar-a-Lago, but you have to be invited to the cocktail receptions for the Achilles Freedom Team of Wounded Veterans or the American Heart Association Gala Luncheon, because these parties are held at private homes in Palm Beach, and even if you have money, you don't get invited unless you measure up to the host's standards. In this regard, Svetlana was still an outsider.

Melanie added the Friesens, Leonard and Muffy, to the guest list, as well. Leonard had married Muffy, his third wife, on the recommendation of the financier, Keith Kleppman, whom he idolized. Kleppman said Muffy reminded him of his own mother. According to Monsignor Klinzing, Muffy had vowed to go once a week to St. Thomas the Martyr Church in West

Palm to wash the feet of homeless men, although she sometimes missed a week or two when foot-washing sessions conflicted with her weekly doubles tennis match at Mar-a-Lago with Bibi Whittaker, Theresa Haas and Michele Roebuck. Muffy never felt entirely comfortable with the arrangement, and after she married Leonard, she often asked herself how many calloused and blistered hooves she'd have to wash to atone for marrying a husband with a billion dollars. Melanie knew that Leonard would do whatever Keith Kleppman did and that, if Keith Kleppman owned a sculpture by Michel Rondelle, the Friesens would compete to buy one, too. In Palm Beach, Kleppman lived next door to Melanie. She would invite him, too.

From the gay community, Melanie invited Alexander Loeb, the fashion mogul, and his companion, Doug. Loeb had been a salesman for a company in Queen's that made men's ties before he figured out how to exploit loopholes in the garment industry's trade agreements with Asian nations. His companies made less profit from their clothing lines than they did from lawsuits against competitors that made knock-offs of his designs. But in the last few years, he'd burned through his fortune and now leased everything that gave him the appearance of wealth, from his house and his cars to his business suits. Even before he'd lost his money, Loeb had been notorious for not paying his bills. He'd stiffed almost every supplier in Palm Beach. Scotti's, the liquor store, would no longer fill his orders; to clean his pool he had to hire a company in Port St. Lucie, about thirty miles away. But alerted by Darius to the rising star in the art firmament of Michel Rondelle, Loeb hoped that he might buy a sculpture and flip it quickly for a profit. "His prices are taking off," Darius told him.

From Mumbai came Mookesh Poonawalla, the property developer, whose network of medical clinics provide door-to-door air and limousine services to the richest women in Asia so that they can enhance their breasts without dirtying their shoes. His wife, Indira, regarded most people in Palm Beach with the same disdain as she held for untouchables in Goa. She also hadn't paid her gardener in six months.

Theresa Haas had married the geriatric founder of a Swiss drug company whose most successful product now kept most people in Palm Beach from going insane and stabbing each other in the neck with a fork. Inheriting his fortune when he died, Theresa now relied on her walker, a pale-skinned, limp-wristed cipher named Digby Winthrop, to accompany her to social events. Theresa cheated so often at bridge that no one would play with her. A recovering alcoholic, she used to carry a mickey of vodka in her purse. Now she carried her dog.

Theresa made no effort to hide her jealousy of Melanie. She was especially covetous of Darius, whose relative youth and masculinity made Digby Winthrop look like a retired female impersonator. Theresa also took offence out of all proportion to the smallest provocation, objecting loudly and slamming her raquet against the net during tennis matches, for example, if she disagreed with a line call, but Melanie decided to tolerate the woman as long as she attended the party with Digby, who was a distant cousin of the Massachusetts Winthrops and had been trained since childhood to remain well-scrubbed and inoffensively elegant in public. Digby was also crazy about reptiles. He kept six small alligators in an aquarium in his condo and collected figures of Komodo dragons modeled in porcelain, paper maché and wood. Melanie figured that he'd fall in love with Michel Rondelle's sculptures, if not with Michel himself, and persuade Theresa to buy one.

To elevate the intellectual tone of her party, Melanie included Professor Sebastian Nevada, the token academic of Palm Beach, whose popular theories about Darwinian economics and social evolution had captured an audience of suburban magazine readers with pretensions of wisdom and an aversion to needless charity and earned him several million dollars in royalties on books like *Conquests of Gifted Leaders* and *I, Me, My: The Three Secrets to Sustainable Greatness*.

Edgar Boyce would bring his latest wife, Blaine. Edgar was so old, he could remember watching the Cleveland Browns win a pro football championship; Blaine was so young that she'd never learned to write with a pen. Whenever she attended a dinner party, she spent most of the evening playing *Words With Friends* on her iPhone. Melanie reminded herself to tell her to turn it off during dinner. Blaine compensated for her stunning dumbness with her genius for assessing a man's fortune. Years ago at a cocktail party, Melanie told her that Hamilton Roebuck, whom Blaine was meeting for the first time, had just inherited five hundred million dollars. "No, he didn't," Blaine said, and she was right. Roebuck had merely inherited the investment portfolio of his late father-in-law, worth a paltry ten million, and Blaine had no interest in men whose net worth amounted to so little.

Whether or not he passed muster with Blaine Boyce, Hamilton Roebuck could still afford to buy one of Dwayne's sculptures, so Melanie put him and his wife on the guest list, as well. Now a patron of the arts, Roebuck had first come to Palm Beach as the personal trainer of a woman whose father owned a high-end vegetable market in Minnesota. Through persistence and marriage, he'd raised enough money to buy out his first father-in-law, then divorced his wife, but kept the store. Ten years later, no one in Palm Beach could remember his first wife's name.

Hamilton had lost count of his wives, but still couldn't resist proposing to women. He loved the courtship, the first kiss, the unadulterated gratitude and happiness that he saw in their eyes when they opened a jewellery box from Van Cleef and Arpels and found a gold engagement ring set with a diamond bigger than a drain plug. Hamilton even loved the planning that went into a wedding. He loved the ceremony, the theatrics, the parties and the honeymoon. After that, though, the love went out of his marriages like water down a toilet. He compared it to playing chess: He got excited by the opening moves, but he felt bewildered by the ensuing complexities and, as the game dragged on, he blamed his wives for enticing him into the match in the first place. After four wives he'd begun to consider celibacy. He'd gone to a few psychiatrists, but it was hard to find one who wasn't as interested as he was in money. The last one had accepted his offer of an E-class Mercedes in return for asking less difficult questions. Hamilton knew he had issues, but money kept the issues at bay as effectively as any doctor. His current wife, Michele, had been a cheerleader for the Dallas Cowboys and had met Hamilton after he'd paid a hundred thousand dollars to sit with her in a Maybach convertible at the Super Bowl parade. She'd been wearing a skin-tight leather cat suit. Within ten days, he'd asked her to marry him.

Benjamin Whittaker and his wife, Bibi, owned a payday lending company with outlets across the Midwest. The company offered cash advances on customers' weekly paychecks, at an annual interest rate of two hundred thirty-five per cent. A subsidiary offered mortgages to high-risk borrowers. Benjamin liked Palm Beach because the place was inaccessible to protesters who blamed him for putting thousands of unqualified borrowers out of their homes after providing them with mortgages that they couldn't afford to service. He didn't want to suffer the same humiliation as his friend in Pasadena, a senior executive with Wells Fargo, who had awakened one morning to find two hundred demonstrators, led by a bearded protestor with a megaphone, milling around under the lemon trees outside his house, chanting obscenities that penetrated the double glazing of his mullioned windows. While several executives of his company had paid hefty fines and spent time in jail for violating securities regulations, Benjamin simply retired and now spent most of his time playing bridge under the name Jimmy Billions.

Whittaker collected vintage Chevrolet Corvettes, with the vague but unarticulated belief that the more Corvettes he owned, the further he could remove himself from death. He now owned forty-seven of them, including a 1963 Grand Sport that he'd bought for six million dollars, and he felt confident that he would never die. So far, he'd been right. In fact, within his circle of friends and acquaintances, death had struck only people who didn't own any Corvettes at all.

His wife, Bibi, had been a society gossip columnist in Palm Beach when they first met, twenty-six years ago. As if to prove that fame and fortune are the currency with which short men attract tall women, Benjamin had married her after he'd put her on retainer to guide him into the heights of Palm Beach society. In return, Bibi introduced Benjamin to a world he'd never known. She also taught him not to smoke cigars at dinner or wear white socks with a blue suit.

Bibi was bony and strangely without definition, like raw bread dough. Her ash-blonde hair seemed weatherproof except for a few wispy clusters like cirrus clouds carefully designed to appear carefree. To make sure that her husband felt at home in Palm Beach, she'd orchestrated an impromptu meeting with the first wife of Doctor Cyrus Beltran, a former Playboy bunny, and paid the woman to fawn over Benjamin. Her seductive swooning convinced Benjamin that his charm exceeded the dimensions of his ego and that Bibi could work miracles.

Although he appeared to have everything a man could want, Benjamin suffered from acute anxiety. If people knew how bad he felt, they might have thought twice about the advantages of wealth. Almost everyone thinks that he'd worry less if he had more money. It makes sense. The less money you have, the more you worry about it. The rent, the mortgage, taxes, gas, insurance, hydro, food, shoes and clothes for the kids, cable TV, a vacation: they all cost money. People worry especially about unexpected bills: repairs to the car; a leak in the roof; a prolonged illness. They see debts approaching like a horde of barbarians. They measure their resources to see if their paychecks will arrive in time to meet the barbarians at the gate. When the onslaught of bills threatens to overwhelm their paltry income, they resort to trickery, sleights of hand and subterfuge – a loan from a relative, a cash advance, an overdraft from the bank, a partial payment on a credit card – that might assuage their creditors with illusions of solvency. Such desperate measures may postpone the day of reckoning, but the attacks never end, and the desperation continues. Year after year they scramble to defend themselves from poverty while they dream of winning a lottery, robbing a bank or inheriting a fortune. If that dream were to come true, they'd pay off their bills once and for all, watch the barbaric debts retreat and worry no more. Or so they think.

They'd be surprised to see how worried the rich can get about their money. In a perpetual state of anxiety, Benjamin Whittaker perspired constantly and often felt short of breath. His fingertips shed their skin like little molting snakes. His bowels churned like an active volcano, and he filled the pockets of his suit jackets with antacid tablets that he swallowed like handfuls of peanuts. Whittaker regarded his anxiety as a weakness. He understood as well as anyone the danger of revealing his vulnerability. After all, he'd built his fortune on exploiting other people's weaknesses, and he knew that his own worries would invite attack. Over the years, he'd mastered his anxiety by using it to fuel his aggression. To most people, he looked as imposing, unruffled and intimidating as ever.

In his mind, however, he couldn't stop thinking about money. More particularly, he couldn't stop thinking of how much money it cost to remain married to Bibi. She was costing him a fortune. The personal chef. The interior designer. The wardrobe consultant. The fitness trainer. The flights back and forth between their homes in New York, London, Aspen and Palm Beach. More than a hundred and fifty thousand a month it cost him to keep Bibi happy. So why wasn't she happy, goddammit?

As Melanie put the finishing touches on her guest list, she turned her attention to the auctioneer for the evening. She knew that an auctioneer with pretensions of royalty would give the other guests more incentive to bid on Michel Rondelle's lizards. With a common variety of gavel-banger, she risked losing her audience completely. She'd learned this lesson from embarrassing experience. At her last dinner party, the guests had ignored the auctioneer, an unimposing little man whose name she couldn't remember, and had drifted away after dinner to the upstairs bathroom, where they'd assembled to watch the O.J. Simpson trial on a TV in the toilet room. They'd come downstairs only after they heard Cyril Gudgeon yelling obscenities at the caged leopard that had clamped its jaws around his arm. Melanie vowed after that to hire an auctioneer whose status would keep her guests from leaving the room. This time she chose the Duke of Hohenzolern-Faustenberg von Spitzbergen, who claimed a distant relationship with Elizabeth, Queen of England. The Duke was known for getting drunk at parties and vomiting on people's shoes. He'd also spent time in a Welsh jail for molesting a minor and now worked for a diamond cartel in Antwerp. But for a fee of ten thousand dollars, the Duke would prime the dinner guests with two hours of enthusiastic chit-chat about the prodigiously talented sculptor Michel Rondelle. And at least he was an authentic aristocrat, unlike that so-called princess who'd bamboozled half the people in Palm Beach a few years ago before she was exposed as a mere commoner from Pittsburgh. To save face, everyone agreed that the woman was mentally ill. Rich people don't feel so gullible if they've been hoodwinked by a whacko.

Putting her list together, Melanie wondered again why so many of them seemed to feel uncomfortable in their own skin. All of them wanted to look like someone else or at least a different, improved version of themselves. Perhaps that explained why Melanie had almost no friends in Palm Beach. How could you have faith in someone's friendship if she secretly wanted to be someone else? No wonder the celebrity industry was booming, Melanie thought. Celebrities had no more character or talent than a cardboard mannequin, but they offered the possibility, without much effort, of a different, improved life, and it seemed to Melanie that almost everyone in America wanted that.

These women wore their wealth like a disguise, Melanie thought, but it wasn't hard to recognize the person they were trying to hide: grasping suburban cheerleaders, shallow as a birdbath, who had calculated their way into their husband's world and proved to the world that they deserved to be there by asserting their second-hand superiority through condescension, as if people in a less exalted position than theirs look at the world through a window smudged with grime that they can't afford to wash off.

What rankled Melanie even more about the clique of wealthy wives in Palm Beach was their persistence in clinging to bourgeois values that rank appearances above substance. In their circle, it's far more important to wear a Valentino jacket to an afternoon tea than it is to spend time with their children. They value punctuality more than kindness. They believe in philanthropy, the more extravagant, the better, but they feel embarrassed by the impulse of simple charity that sometimes haunts them when they watch their gardeners kneeling in their flowerbeds or hear that the housemaid's daughter had cancer. The impulse to extend charity is an irrelevant reminder of a previous life, a vestigial remnant, like men's breasts, that no longer has any useful function.

Whenever she encountered such people, Melanie went out of her way to piss them off. She enjoyed nothing more than disrupting the daisy chain of sanctimonious butt-kissing that prevails in their Palm Beach society. She once erected a marquee on her property, the kind you set up for a big wedding, but instead of using it for a dinner or dance, she used it to house a busload of homeless people. She bought them all nylon training suits, fed them three meals a day and let them play soccer behind her guest house. She even invited a masseuse to attend to them. The town finally ordered her to take it down after her neighbors complained. "Like a fucking refugee camp," said her neighbor, Keith Kleppman. Melanie could hardly wait to take these people's money in return for a wooden lizard.

Melanie thought about removing Kleppman, from the guest list. She regarded him as a pompous bully who thought that money absolved him of all responsibility to be human. But, as Darius reminded her, the success of the auction depended on Kleppman's appetite for expensive art.

Kleppman started his first company when he was twenty-three with en-velopes of cash given to him by his father, a protegé of Meyer Lansky and a compulsive high-stakes gambler and jewel fence, who laundered mon-ey raised from drugs, prostitution, extortion and bookmaking for the top bosses of the New York underworld. Initially, Keith Kleppman Investment Securities LLC made money trading penny stocks on the over-the-counter market, circulating rumors about imminent windfalls and then selling the stocks before their inflated prices came back to earth. As the years passed, Kleppman nudged, shoved, muscled, cheated and connived his way into every nook and cranny of his father's business. By the time I started writing this story, KKIS was managing more than eighty billion dollars, primarily for offshore clients that included the Russian mafia, Middle Eastern arms dealers and Latin-American drug cartels, and Keith Kleppman believed that he had been ordained by God from childhood to carry the responsibilities and burdens of wealth. Last year, for a hundred thousand dollars, Klep-pman bought his way into a sold-out New Year's Eve celebration at Mar-a-Lago with the U.S. President. He recently paid a quarter of a million dollars for a cryogenic chamber in Arizona that will keep his body frozen after he dies until he can be resurrected like Lazarus by some miracle of modern medicine. "Bad enough he has to live once," Melanie says.

From his perch on top of a pile of money, Kleppman fancied himself a visionary of the global financial world. He modeled himself after Henry Kissinger, upon whose inflated ego a former United States President had risen to power. He carried himself with the same gravitas and cultivated the same statesman-like basso profundo tone, which rumbled like thunder from deep within his chest. When people questioned the morality of his finan-cial dealings with murderers, extortionists and corrupt regimes that gassed their own citizens with chemical weapons, he reminded them that innocent people had suffered because of Kissinger's advice to Richard Nixon to win peace with honor in Viet Nam by dropping napalm on villages of women and children. "Great men make tough decisions," Kleppman said over the half-glasses that he perched on the end of his nose to give himself a pro-fessorial air. Like Kissinger, Kleppman played with toy soldiers to re-enact famous battles, and he slept well at night knowing that he shouldered Napo-leonic burdens without allowing emotion to cloud his judgment. It pleased him to know, as well, that he had far more money than that gasbag Henry Kissinger.

Kleppman's house next door had taken five years to build. To clear the site, he'd torn down three houses that had overlooked the Atlantic Ocean for more than half a century. Two of them had been designed by Addison Mizner, a big, gay, unschooled architect, who specialized in designing pink stucco palaces that incorporated arcades, wrought-iron balconies, precast rococo mouldings and roofs of terra-cotta tile manufactured by his factory in West Palm Beach. Kleppman bought all three houses for eighty-five million dollars, tore them down and replaced them with a sprawling pile that was as big as a velodrome. It contained a three-lane bowling alley, a shooting range and a virtual-reality games room where Kleppman conducted war maneuvers with his toy soldiers. The garage accommodated seven cars. Kleppman named the house Villa Patrizia, after his wife, whom he divorced soon after they moved in.

By the time the house was finished, his neighbors had sued him more often than they'd said hello to him. That's not so unusual among the people of Palm Beach. They hire lawyers to file lawsuits the way they hire maids to make their beds. Theresa Haas, the pharmaceutical heiress, sued her hairdresser for revealing to Muffy Friesen that she'd dyed her roots.

The latest round of suits and counter-suits began when Kleppman let his King Charles spaniels run through Melanie's flowerbeds, leaving their disgusting little turds to petrify in the sunshine near her muhly grass. By allowing his dogs to lay siege to her lawn and gardens, Kleppman might as well have attacked Melanie's surrogate family.

Kleppman intended to install a helicopter landing pad on the roof of his house and instructed a team of lawyers to push his plan through the local council. He might have succeeded if his property didn't lie within the flight path of Palm Beach Airport and if a no-fly zone hadn't surrounded Mar-a-Lago, the President's vacation property at the time. When Kleppman discovered that helicopters were forbidden from entering the air space above his house and would likely have been shot down on sight, he weighed his options, which included buying the airport and mounting a campaign to ensure the President lost the next election. Eventually he dropped his plan for a helicopter and bought a Donzi cigarette boat instead.

Less than six months after the house was finished, the Kleppmans began renovating the place. They added outbuildings, removed trees and planted new ones. They applied for variances on height limitations and beach access. Trucks and bulldozers ran constantly onto their property, leaving clods of earth and debris strewn across the blacktop of South Ocean Boulevard and onto the manicured fringes of their neighbors' lawns. At one point, a construction crew accidentally punctured a water main, flooding the road and forcing the town to shut off service for almost a day.

The Kleppmans marked the perimeter of their property with a fully grown ficus hedge as forbidding and impenetrable as the walls of a penitentiary. Through an opening carved through the hedge, a driveway ran from South Ocean Boulevard across a manicured lawn to a portico at the south end of the house and then continued past a two-story garage to a seven-bedroom guest house that overlooked Lake Worth. To pave the driveway, they shipped to Palm Beach sixteen truckloads of finely crushed gravel from a meteorite that had landed in a field of soya beans near Cleveland. The gravel was highly valued because it shed no dust. The Kleppmans could afford to indulge their profound aversion to dirt.

Through one of his subsidiary companies, he sponsored a wildlife series that publicized the plight of endangered animals. This entitled him to a tax credit for the licence fee that he paid to shoot them. Stuffed and mounted in a climate-controlled pavilion behind the guest house, he displayed a lion, a tiger, a water buffalo, an elephant and a rhinoceros. The place of honor was occupied by a polar bear. "Not many of those fuckers in Palm Beach," he'd say after he'd watched a guest's jaw drop at the sight of it. "Cost me twenty thousand dollars for the licence."

The Kleppmans installed pieces from their art collection inside the main house. These included a Rothko, a Brancusi and a weird funhouse of mirrors by Yayoi Kusama. They'd acquired many of these pieces on the advice of Darius Pierre. When the Kleppmans finally finished their house, Keith divorced his wife.

Considering his acrimonious dealings with his neighbors, you might wonder why Keith Kleppman continued his relationship with Darius. But Kleppman never let the pandemonium of emotion interfere with his single-minded pursuit of a good deal. If Darius offered to sell him a work of art whose value would increase enough to triple his investment, why should he quibble over personal animosities?

There was another reason why Kleppman couldn't abandon Darius so easily. Darius had introduced him to the less salubrious side of life in Palm Beach. Through Darius, he'd become a regular at strip clubs like Ultra and Runway 69. He'd met Shirko, the most reliable importer in Palm Beach of exotic fruits, vegetables and cocaine. Darius had also introduced Kleppman to a teenager from West Palm Beach named Mary Louise Hobsbawn. In return for concert tickets, designer jeans, iPhones and cash, Mary Louise enlisted young girls to entertain Kleppman's important contacts at his all-night parties in the guest house. Sometimes Darius attended the parties, too. To get there, he just walked through an opening in the hedge that separated Melanie's property from Villa Patrizia.

Five

On the day before the party, Melanie's designer, Alain, called from his shop on Worth Avenue to tell her that the dress she'd ordered had arrived from Milan. Melanie told him to bring it to the house. But when she tried it on, the dress, crafted from embroidered silk-lined leather, made her feel uneasy. It was modeled after a dress worn by a celebrity named Kylie Jenner, and it seemed a bit risqué for Palm Beach. Its tight bodice accentuated her breasts and hinted at her nipples, and the mauve fabric caressed her hips and hugged the curve of her buttocks. She felt embarrassed when she tried it on and quickly dropped it onto the floor, replacing it with another one that she'd bought in New York and hadn't yet worn this season. But then she changed her mind again and settled on the mauve leather dress. She still didn't like what she saw in the mirror, and she wasn't sure if the fault lay with the dress or with herself. To avoid making a judgment, she took a pill and let herself off the hook.

That afternoon, Melanie's team of Mexican gardeners cut the grass twice, from east to west and north to south, with greens mowers, then swept it with brooms. The next morning, a team of professional movers rolled Melanie's matching Bosendorfer pianos into the formal dining room. Darius positioned Michel Rondelle's lizards on their closed lids under revolving pinlights in the ceiling, which animated the jewels and seemed to breathe life into the mahogany creatures. Next to one he placed an embossed card that said, ""Madam Butterfly doesn't play the air guitar, 2017."

Later that morning, Melanie's staff placed round tables near the water's edge overlooking Lake Worth, covered with Dupioni silk harvested from double cocoons that infused the hand-woven fabric with iridescent orange, mauve and chartreuse tones. As the guests arrived that evening at sunset, they remarked on the way the colors on the wide horizon complemented the tablecloths. From inside the house, Billy Joel sang *Movin' Out*.

For most of the guests, Melanie's party was a social triumph, marketing exercise and business opportunity. For me, it was part of my job. Since I couldn't further their ambitions, I knew they wouldn't waste their time making small talk with me. Among themselves, they talked about nothing, a talent that I've never mastered. On this talent for hiding deadly serious intentions behind a veil of banalities, corporate empires have risen and fallen. Men who had just made billion-dollar deals to float a share issue or sell a molybdenum mine in Nigeria yammered away about their dogs or their most recent dinner at Buccan.

I walked across the grass toward the lake, nodding as I passed the infinity pool toward Digby Winthrop, who hovered at the shoulder of Theresa Haas while checking his two smartphones for messages. I'd met Digby several times, and we'd cultivated an acquaintanceship of gestures: nodding, raising eyebrows, shoulder shrugs and head-shakes. With jeweled fingers, Theresa tickled the head of her vicious-looking chihuahua as she talked to Indira Poonawalla, then turned her attention to the doorway as Doctor Cyrus Beltran emerged in his Panama hat into the evening air with his wife, Svetlana, wearing a pair of over-sized sunglasses. Svetlana adjusted the plunging neckline of her dress, determined to make her new breasts do what she'd paid for them to do, and they all made their way across the lawn.

I moved off to photograph the Whittakers as they joined Hamilton Roebuck and his new wife, Michele, near one of the iguana displays. The Roebucks had just returned from their honeymoon in Morocco, but I could see from his posture that Hamilton had already lost interest in his latest wife. After a few drinks tonight, he would hardly remember her name. Maybe that's why she spent so much money on surgery, trying to keep a face that her husband would recognize.

"I'm through with Marrakesh," said Michele.

"We prefer Amanjena," said Bibi Whittaker, who actually preferred smoking cigars in the company of men to vapid chit-chat with idle women. "The bathrooms are delicious."

"Amanjena's not the same since the Russian took over," said Svetlana Beltran, as she and her husband joined the group. She rested her hand on Hamilton's arm. He turned his head and stared at her breasts.

Michele said, "Arab men go for overweight blondes."

Hamilton forced a smile. "One look at Michele and I had to beat them off with a stick," he said.

"I suspect she can defend herself, Hamilton," said Bibi Whittaker.

"Hnyaw, nyaw, nyaw," Hamilton Roebuck snorted. "Fabulous."

"I prefer Saudi men," said Michele. "They have more money."

"Hnyaw, nyaw, nyaw," her husband snorted again. "Fabulous."

"Best food in the world," said Benjamin Whittaker. "In Riyadh. Terrific food. Unbelievable hummus. Really terrific."

"I'd like to live in a country like Riyadh," said Svetlana Beltran.

"Why's that, honey?" said Doctor Cyrus Beltran.

She pursed her lips. Her sunglasses moved from side to side like bug eyes as she shook her head. "It would be so nice to live in a place where there are no poor people."

"But darling," said Bibi Whittaker, "how would you clean your house?"

"You can't escape from poverty," said Sebastian Nevada, the best-selling academic, who had joined the conversation after arguing briefly with his wife on the patio. He tilted his head back and raised his left arm, as if he was delivering a lecture to a room of enthralled graduate students. His wife, Paula, had retreated to a nearby table and now focused her attention on her smartphone, which she used to play *Words With Friends*. A former professor of marketing at Stanford's business school, she had lost all affection for her husband after his series of affairs with his female PhD students, and she saw no point in engaging in social conversation with people whose intellectual refinement fell far short of hers.

"It's my experience, based on first-hand research," Professor Nevada intoned, "that the world seeps in through the economic interstices, gags you with the stench of rotting flesh, chokes you on the blood of innocent victims, shames you until you wish you'd never taken your first breath, just for being human and alive. You have a facelift and a tummy tuck, and the world feels like a better place for a while. You buy two new cars, you replace the lawn furniture, you fly to Monaco, but somehow the world catches up with you. You can't escape."

His audience stared at him as they tried to make sense of his observations, until Michele Roebuck, said, "Yes, but poverty is no excuse for bad taste."

"How true," said Svetlana. She raked her gaze over Bibi Whittaker's dress and remarked silently on the larger woman's fat armpits.

Nearby, Leonard Friesen leaned against a Jean Arp sculpture on the lawn, sucking on a cigarette. He wore a pink sports jacket with pants of peacock-blue linen and shoes of soft green suede with gold buckles. The shoes, like furry animals adorned with jewellery, were intended less for walking than for drawing attention to his feet. One of the close-up magicians wandered past and pulled an egg from Leonard's breast pocket.

"Leonard shot a rhinoceros," said Muffy Friesen, patting her red hair.

"Bigger than Kleppman's," said Leonard.

"In the jungle?" said Suzy Hornbeam. She bent her lips into the shape of a smile as she cast her eyes around the garden to find someone more important than Muffy to talk to.

"No, dear," said Muffy, "from a helicopter. "It cost him fifty thousand dollars."

"Worth every goddam penny," Leonard said. He pulled his wife against him and grabbed his crotch.

"Got the old hormones pumping, boy. You'll never know how it feels to stare death in the face . . ."

"Oh, sweetie," said Muffy.

"I'm surprised you could see his face from the helicopter," said Suzy Hornbeam.

A waiter approached with a tray of martinis. Suzy handed her empty glass to the waiter, took a full one and lurched across the lawn toward the Whittakers, the Beltrans and the Roebucks. Inside the house, Billy Joel sang "Honesty."

Benjamin Whittaker looked different tonight. He'd worn a pair of custom-made elevator shoes that added two inches to his height, and he had a full head of hair, woven for thirty-five thousand dollars from the tresses of Egyptian women into a second scalp attached to his head.

Oscar Hornbeam glanced toward his departing wife, then whispered, "I always take a hooker to bed while I'm in Africa. Preferably a black one." He hurried after Suzy before she stumbled and spilled her martini on the grass.

From across the lawn, Alexander Loeb stared at Leonard Friesen. "Shoots big game," he said to his companion, Doug.

"And marries big tits," said Doug.

Moving among the guests, Melanie and Darius passed Keith Kleppman, who reached out and patted Melanie's butt as she walked by. "Nicest ass in the crowd," he lied. Melanie resisted the urge to turn and plant her knee in his crotch the way she'd learned in her self-defence course.

They approached the Whittakers, who were discussing Keith Kleppman's art collection.

"Kleppman wouldn't know a Kandinsky from a Kleenex box," said Bibi Whittaker.

"I've been to Kandinsky's," said Michele Roebuck.

"What happened to your hair, Benjamin?" Suzy Hornbeam said as she joined the group. She swallowed her fifth martini in a single gulp.

Some of the guests began moving into the dining room. Mookesh

Poonawalla talked to his wife, Indira, about Billy Joel. "He used to live with Cindy Crawford," he said, running his fingers over the polished maple of one of the Bosendorfers. When his wife looked perplexed, he said, "The famous model?" A close-up magician stopped beside Indira and lifted a silver dollar from behind her ear. She scowled.

Six little people in black satin livery circulated through the room carrying rotating trays of German salads, rare caviars, mushrooms and other dainty delicacies. The chef had prepared them in homage to Catherine the Great, who had served these Russian zakuski to her guests with small glasses of vodka.

"I heard that Michel Rondelle is an idiot savant," said Suzy Hornbeam, leaning against Digby Winthrop as they moved into the dining room.

"Apparently, he can do trigonometry in his head," said Digby.

By the door, the Duke of Hohenzolern-Faustenberg von Spitzbergen sipped on a large bourbon. In his other hand he held a mound of shrimp on a cocktail napkin. He looked toward one of the sculptures on the piano. "Is that a fucking Giacometti?"

Suzy Hornbeam introduced herself to the Duke. "Suzy Hornbeam, je m'appelle," she said. She offered her hand to the Duke.

With his hands full, the Duke clicked his heels together and inclined his head stiffly. A close-up magician plucked an egg from his shirt collar.

Suzy explained to the Duke that she had connections to France and that her husband had made his fortune in car parts. "And what do you do, Duke?"

"I collect," he said.

"Nous aussi," said Suzy, who took another martini from a waiter. "My great grandfather collected Picassos."

"That would have been in the 1940s?" said the Duke.

"My family goes back much further than that."

"To the early Renaissance, I'm sure," said the Duke. "You have that look about you."

"And what look would that be, Duke?"

"The look of enlightened humanism."

"The look of six martinis," said her husband. He plucked the glass from his wife's fingers.

In anger, Suzy said, "Where does this guy Darius get off charging so much for these goddam sculptures?"

"Calm down, Suzy," said Oscar.

"I'm serious. Look at this shit." She gestured toward a lizard on the nearest piano. "Who'd pay thirty thousand dollars for that?"

Muffy Friesen said one of Dwayne's lizards would fit nicely into their penthouse in the Trump Tower. The pavé would complement the flecked green wallpaper in the library, she said.

"I didn't think you could fit a library into that little place of yours," said Bibi Whittaker..

"We saw your library, Muffy," said Michele Roebuck, "in that Journal article."

"The one where Leonard was holding the book upside down," said Suzy Hornbeam.

Cyrus Beltran laughed.

"That was our little joke," said Muffy. "It only works with friends who can read."

Billy Joel started singing "Just the Way You Are."

"I read a book the other day," said Leonard Friesen, a short fat man who took himself too seriously and felt threatened and angry if anyone made a joke at his expense.

"A book of matches?" said Suzy.

She turned to listen to one of the little people who had stopped to talk to her. A moment later, she laughed out loud, stood up straight and knocked the tray out of the little man's hand, spilling caviar and mushroom caps over the shoes of Svetlana Beltran.

"Esti d'épais de marde!," Svetlana muttered, assuming no one but she would understand the vile expression. But Melanie did.

"Mon vieux, je parle francais aussi," she said, "mais moi, je parle comme un Francais de France."

"Do you think they're Fijian crested iguanas?" said Blaine Boyce, leaning closer to examine one of the jeweled lizards.

Above the din in the room, the butler announced the arrival of Michel Rondelle and Mary Louise Hobsbawn. From the entrance to the room, Mike directed his eyes toward the glass doors that led into the garden. Holding his face in a rigid half-smile, he stood in the doorway like an intrepid explorer, studying the crowd as he prepared to plunge onward into the interior of this new-found land. A magician appeared beside him and lifted a quarter from behind his ear. Startled, Mike cocked his fist, preparing to punch him, but the magician had wisely darted out of his reach.

Cyrus Beltran looked toward the new arrivals. Mary Louise had dyed her hair black and let it spread across her bare shoulders. She'd bought her embroidered leather party dress at Goodwill, in West Palm Beach. It was almost identical to Melanie's but far more flattering to an adolescent figure like hers. It took a moment before Cyrus Beltran recognized Mary Louise from one of Kleppman's bacchanals. He pulled his Panama hat down lower over his eyes and turned away. "Where did that little waiter go?" he said, and he scurried toward the other end of the room.

Like a lifeguard executing a rescue, Darius stepped between Mike and Mary Louise and led them into the dining room. He introduced them to the Whittakers and the Friesens as "the artist and his muse."

"He doesn't look like an artist," said Svetlana Beltran to Hamilton Roebuck, but Roebuck, too, had recognized Mary Louise and had knelt down beside one of the little waiters to ask him where he bought his clothes. Even kneeling down, he was taller than the waiter, who wondered why a guest would even talk to him let alone ask him questions about his wardrobe.

When the butler announced dinner, the guests made their way to their places at the tables spread throughout the dining room under a Chihuly chandelier, which hung from the ceiling like a psychedelic gondola. The tables of six were set with silver, gold, porcelain and crystal and centered with a tall trumpet vase filled with kumquats, baby lemons, limes, grapes and oranges.

"Gardeners here are so good with plants," said Bibi Whittaker as she admired the centerpiece on her table. "Ours has a mystical relationship with the acanthus."

"That's because he's from Peru," said Oscar Hornbeam.

At each place, a gold fingerbowl held a black pearl in Provencal spring water. The Wedgwood dishes had once belonged to Catherine the Great, and a Parisian silversmith had manufactured the cutlery in 1873.

On their chairs, the guests found the monograph prepared by Darius Pierre about the artist, Michel Rondelle. "Often compared to Jean-Michel Basquiat and Daumier Rousseau," it said, "Rondelle grew up on a First Nations reserve in Canada, the son of a gravestone engraver from Mississippi and an Iroquois mother who was a cousin of the indigenous painter Norval Morisseau. With guidance from his father but no formal training, Rondelle honed his innate talent by imitation and application. As a teenager, he spent a year in prison for selling marijuana to an undercover agent of the RCMP and refusing to identify his supplier. In prison, a sympathetic art counselor recognized the boy's skill as a draughtsman and provided him with tools, wood and instruction. It was a turning point in his emerging identity as a sculptor.

"Upon his release, Rondelle traveled to Spain with an introduction to the sculptor Juan Muñoz. Muñoz accommodated the boy at his home near Madrid, allowing him to serve as his apprentice on some of the Spanish sculptor's best-known works including The Wasteland and Double Bind, now installed at Tate Modern.

"After seven years, Rondelle struck out on his own. With Muñoz's encouragement, he worked at a relentless pace, as if he had some foreknowledge that his life would end tragically and prematurely, like other luminaries such as Jim Morrison, Janis Joplin, Jimi Hendrix and Jean-Michel Basquiat. Between the ages of twenty-four and twenty-seven, Rondelle produced more than one hundred and fifty works before he was kidnapped by Basque terrorists and had a near-death encounter with a bull in Pamplona.

"Thanks to the gallerist Darius Pierre, the reputation of Michel Rondelle has been restored and his career resurrected. After re-emerging onto the art scene last year at Art Basel Hong Kong, Rondelle has attracted interest from collectors such as Estrellita Brodsky, Jorge Pérez, Canadian billionaire Michael Wekerle and the musician Sting, while his pieces have climbed steadily higher in value."

Even though no one would read beyond the last sentence of that paragraph, Darius had appended to the monograph two incomprehensible essays written by reputable art critics, who'd owed him a favor. He added a few endorsements of Rondelle's work from prominent museum professionals in Los Angeles and New York, along with some canned quotations from the artist himself:

"Muñoz told me that two things are impossible to represent: the present and death, and the only way to arrive at them is by their absence."

"I agree with Tino Sehgal when he says that it's not about rich and poor. I'm much more concerned with the presumptions of this poor or rich thing. The rich and poor divide is for me very material. And of course material is not the most important site of substance."

And in case no one at the auction read through the entire opening paragraph, Darius had repeated the final sentence on another page:

"Since Rondelle's work caused a sensation last year at Art Dubai, its value has climbed steadily higher."

Mike leaned forward to catch the eye of Darius Pierre. "Who wrote this shit?" he said.

"Me," said Darius. "Good, isn't it?"

Their conversation attracted the attention of the Whittakers and several other people seated near them. Mike just nodded. "Sure," he said.

Apart from a shadowy photograph of the artist, everything in the booklet was a lie. But that didn't matter. As Darius would explain later, the words in the monograph meant less to the people in his market than the monograph itself. Its weight and the dense quality of its hand-crafted paper conveyed authority and high status. To produce it, Darius had hired a company in Fort Lauderdale. The company designed lavish brochures for real-estate agents that portrayed high-end houses in the same enticing way as Victoria's Secret portrays women's underpants.

Initially, Darius had wondered about including so many words on each page, since no one in the room tonight really cared about the artist enough to read more than a few words about him. But even if they cared only about the price, potential buyers in the room tonight needed to feel as if they were paying for the art's intrinsic value, and the perfect-bound monograph confirmed by its weight and texture that Mike's work was valuable indeed.

At the table next to Mike, Hamilton Roebuck reached for the wine bottle and filled his own glass but no one else's. Cyrus Beltran sat with his back to the head table. He invested in art to complement the vision of his cosmetic dental practice, he said, and took an appropriate tax deduction on each investment. "It's the intersection of beauty," he said, "which my clients want, and art, which their fees allow me to buy. But I like my art to make me feel good. I don't want my art to make me feel depressed."

"How do you feel about your clients?" said Suzy Hornbeam. Cyrus adjusted his hat and pretended that he hadn't heard the question.

"There's enough depression in the world," said Theresa Haas, the pharmaceutical heiress. From the handbag in her lap the head of her chihuahua emerged to nip at a piece of carpaccio that she held in her fingertips.

A team of slender, blonde Norwegian servers emerged from the kitchen. Benoit had hired them from a modeling agency in Miami, on Melanie's specifications. Melanie knew the men would bid more aggressively on Michel Rondelle's sculptures if they could impress an attractive woman in a short skirt and red stilettoes who wasn't their wife. The servers placed bowls of sturgeon and champagne soup in front of each guest, then took a pace back and stood behind the men's chairs.

"Catherine the Great's favorite," said Melanie to Keith Kleppman, who was admiring the Norwegian servers. "Grigory Potemkin once sold a Tintoretto to buy the ingredients."

"Russians buy anything if it's cheap," said Kleppman.

"Is there salt in this soup?" Svetlana Beltran asked her husband. "I don't eat salt."

"Just eat it, Svetlana," he said from under the brim of his Panama hat.

At the end of the head table, Mary Louise said, "How much do you think this house cost?"

"We don't talk about money, dear," said Muffy Friesen, who imagined herself initiating this raw, unsophisticated adolescent into the more refined world of Palm Beach society, "like Pygmalion and Galileo," she said later to her husband.

Seated beside the artist, Benjamin Whittaker leaned closer to Mike to examine his second-hand suit jacket. "I had one just like that," Benjamin said.

"Goodwill," said Mike. "Thirty bucks."

Billy Joel played a slow version of "Uptown Girl" as another team of blonde servers delivered an intermediate course of Dviena sterlet, an over-fished species of sturgeon from the Caspian Sea, in champagne sauce. Next came a course of chicken in crème fraiche, mayonnaise, lime juice and zest, followed by partridge. Each course was served with exquisite reverence, elegantly and without noise, as if the guests were receiving the body of the Messiah from priestesses in a cult of prosperity.

The blonde waitresses filled wine glasses and fetched harder drinks for guests who preferred them. Melanie had arranged with the Duke of Hohenzolern-Faustenberg von Spitzbergen to conduct an open auction for Dwayne's lizards, but she wanted to make sure the guests had drunk enough before he called for the first bid.

"Drunk and horny," she told the Duke. "Wait till they're drunk and horny."

From the head table, she watched Suzy Hornbeam as she took the pearl from her finger bowl and drank the water.

When dinner ended, bidding on the sculptures started at twenty-five thousand dollars. Hamilton Roebuck raised the bidding, followed by Leonard Friesen. By the time Benjamin Whittaker opened his eyes and hollered, bids had reached forty thousand dollars. As the bidding continued, he would have raised his offer, but his wife restrained him. "They're just lizards," Bibi said. "We have dogs. We don't have room for lizards."

The bidding ended only when Leonard Friesen had raised the price by another twenty thousand dollars. Now he beamed at Keith Kleppman at the head table, noticing with a shock of pride that he'd worn the same silk suspenders as his idol. "You've blazed a trail, Keith," he hollered. "Again!"

Kleppman raised a hand in modest benediction.

When the auction ended, Melanie announced that the sale of Michel Rondelle's work had raised more than a quarter of a million dollars in support of the Fijian crested iguana. Leonard Friesen had bid on all the sculptures, but succeeded in buying only three. Benjamin Whittaker had fallen asleep again and looked disappointed when he woke up. Observing his disappointment, Doctor Cyrus Beltran offered to give him the sculpture that he'd acquired. When Benjamin shook his head, the dentist became insistent until Benjamin erupted. "Don't bully me, Cyrus," he said.

"He's just being generous, dear," said Bibi Whittaker.

"That's not generosity," said Benjamin, who became irritable when he awoke from a nap. "This prick gives you a gift and insists you like it. I don't even like fucking lizards."

When dinner ended, Melanie introduced Al Gore, a venture capitalist and former vice-president of the United States, who spoke, to everyone's relief, for less than five minutes. When he finished, he thanked Melanie for inviting him, then hurried with his assistant out of the room. The guests stirred in their chairs and began to stand up. Digby Winthrop weaved past Michel Rondelle at the head table. As he passed, he stuck a business card into Michel's breast pocket "Call me," he said. "I love talking to sensitive men."

He started toward the back of the house, then turned around. "We're going to the pool," he said. "Come join us if you like. The night's still young."

After dinner, Barry Manilow sang "Mandy", "Copacabana" and "I Write the Songs", accompanied by five musicians on drums, guitar, violin, saxophone and harp. Benjamin Whittaker had recovered his energy and, despite his liver spots and tremors, began to flirt outrageously. "Come to my house," he said, holding his lips against Indira Poonawalla's ear as they cha-chaed. "I'll show you how a real man takes care of a woman in this country."

Indira looked around the room for her husband, but Mookesh had gone outside with Suzy Hornbeam to help her find her purse. From the airport on the other side of the lake, the bright light of a jet ascended into the sky, followed by a sound like thunder.

"Great fun, Melanie," hollered Alexander Loeb, flashing his whitened teeth as he watched his companion, Doug, whirling Theresa Haas around the dance floor. Digby Winthrop had returned from the pool and waded through a throng of dancers until he reached Doug. He pushed his wet hair back from his forehead and said, "I know you're a friend of mine, but I just want you to know one thing. This is my girl, and I own her." Doug looked at him, then turned away with Theresa in his arms as if he'd heard nothing but the sound of a bird flapping its wings.

Professor Sebastian Nevada raised Mary Louise's hand over her head and watched her twirl in her tight leather dress under his arm. His wife watched them dancing for a moment, then walked out of the room.

Having found her purse, Suzy Hornbeam stood beside Michel Rondelle while her husband took their photograph with his iPhone. Doctor Cyrus Beltran, keeping his back to Mary Louise as she danced with the professor, adjusted his fedora and said, "How do you achieve such economy of motion?"

"Not sure what you mean," said Mike.

"August Lizard, for example," Beltran said. "It contains such force, as if it's poised to leap out of itself."

"Did you go to the Slade?" said the Duke of Hohenzolern-Faustenberg von Spitzbergen.

"The Slade?" said Mike.

"The art school, darling," said Melanie Merriwether, taking Mike's arm and leading him away. A beady-eyed, rat-faced character with a bad haircut and cheap scuffed shoes hovered by Mike's shoulder. "I'm curious about the name," he said. "*Madam Butterfly Doesn't Play the Air Guitar.* Are you making a sly reference to the cultural dichotomy of western civilization's class consciousness?"

"Whatever," said Mike.

Melanie led the way along the hall to the double staircase that ascended to the second floor. The pesky man persisted. "Bernard Berenson, the Harvard-trained art historian, told Isabella Stewart Gardner that he didn't want her to buy a brace of Rembrandts, like any vulgar millionaire. What do you say now that a collector has just bought three of your pieces tonight? And how do you justify your prices?"

"Better than ten bucks," Mike said.

Assuming he was joking, the man laughed, then lobbed more questions at Mike, each one wrapped in convoluted digressions like darts in cotton batting.

Finally, Melanie took Mike's hand. "That's enough," she said. "I want this man to myself."

"Who was that?" Mike said as they walked up the stairs.

"The art critic for the Miami Herald," said Melanie.

"Glorious evening, Melanie," Bibi Whittaker called out from the foyer. Her husband tried to find Doctor Cyrus Beltran to tell him he would accept his offer of a lizard after all, but he discovered that Beltran had gone next door to join Kleppman's party.

Outside, in the garden, the sky was deep green. In the shadows, Darius Pierre stripped off his clothes, ran across the lawn and dived naked into the pool, with Digby Winthrop hot on his heels. Hamilton Roebuck looked at Svetlana Beltran, who had followed him outside. "Melanie's resident art dealer," he said, placing his hand against her bare back.

Some guests lingered, but most of the women had started edging their partners toward the front door, hoping to be in bed by ten so they'd be well rested for their morning Pilates classes and toning rituals with their personal trainers. A few of the husbands sent their wives home alone, explaining that they'd agreed to meet next door with Keith Kleppman.

"Meeting," Melanie muttered. "That's a euphemism."

Upstairs, Melanie lay on her bed. The walls of her bedroom shimmered in the room's soft lighting. They'd been papered with the iridescent wings of butterflies from Brazil. Sounds from the departing guests filtered into the room.

"Wonderful evening."

"Watch your step, Oscar."

"I shouldn't have had that last glass of wine."

"Men think they have sex appeal," said the voice of Bibi Whittaker. "But women aren't interested in sex. All they want from men is babies and security. Men are just too stupid to know it."

"You can stay with me if you like," Melanie said to Mike.

⊙

After frolicking in the pool with Digby Winthrop, Darius pulled himself onto the deck and dried himself off with a white towel. "See you soon, pool boy," he said to Digby, who remained in the water.

Theresa Haas appeared at the edge of the pool with Digby's trousers in her hand. She dropped them on the deck and said, "This isn't part of our arrangement, Digby."

"I was rather carried away," Digby said, holding his chin above the water.

"Come on," said Theresa. "We haven't got all night."

Darius went into the house to find Melanie. He walked up the stairs past a Piet Mondrian painting on the landing. From the far end of the hall, he heard the faint sounds of a guitar over the pulsing thud of a drum. When he pushed open the heavy oak door of Melanie's bedroom, Mike was alone on the bed. He looked at Darius and smiled.

"Want to join us?" he said.

"She won't be back," said Darius.

He took a wad of cash from his pocket and counted fifteen one-hundred-dollar bills. He tossed them onto the bed. "Here," he said. "Take it. It's yours."

Mike looked at the cash, but he didn't pick it up. Darius moved to the closet. The double oak doors were closed, but he knew that Melanie was inside. Melanie went there whenever she felt threatened by the world. Secluded in the closet, Melanie felt safe. She could reduce her world to the one person she trusted without reservation and admired without qualification: herself.

When Darius opened the doors, the music assaulted him like a punch in the face.

"Bow down to her on Sunday, salute her when her birthday comes," sang Bob Dylan.

The closet was as big as a squash court, and the mirrored walls and ceiling gave it infinite dimensions. There was a carpet in the middle of the floor and a chair with a table where Melanie had put her glass. There were floor-to-ceiling mirrors on each wall.

Inspired by Dylan's lyrics, Melanie wore an Egyptian ring and had instructed her decorator to find a beaten-up brass trumpet and an antique bass drum, which lay on the carpet under a rack of dresses. He'd searched through antique shops and jumble sales until he found both items in Paris. The trumpet had belonged to the jazz musician Chet Baker. He'd used it to record "My Funny Valentine" just before he died. The drum had been played by a sergeant major in the Marine Corps Bugle Band in a parade on VE Day.

Darius closed the doors behind him. Melanie looked at his reflection and felt some relief. For a moment, until she remembered that she'd paid for it, she could feel love in her life. For Melanie, love was a service delivered by others for a price.

Everyone in Melanie's life performed a function: South Americans who came from the jungle and were good with plants; French chefs who prepared her meals; Mexicans who kept her house clean. And then there was her Jewish divorce lawyer. She depended on Darius to accompany her to events when she didn't want to appear alone. She depended on him, as well, to serve as a target for her anger. When she felt dissatisfied, disillusioned, vulnerable or despairing, she could focus her resentment on Darius, knowing that he would do his job and accept it without retaliation. But neither Darius nor these other people really counted. They were as interchangeable as coffee cups. If one of them let her down, she could pay another one to do her bidding. Friends were a dime a dozen. People would do anything for money, even love her.

Darius told me he felt sorry for Melanie. Sometimes, he allowed himself to confuse his pity with love. He knew better than anyone why she struggled against the world, why she felt as if she might drown if she didn't swim constantly against its tides until, like tonight, she broke down in exhaustion. She'd learned from her father that the world was a cruel, disappointing and demanding place and that it showed no mercy. During the Second World

War, her father had escaped death by servicing Russian naval officers in return for their protection of him and his mother as they tried to make their way to America from Tashkent. But the officers had let the young man down. Waiting in Turkmenbashi to cross the Caspian Sea, he'd been restrained by a gang of Soviet criminals called suki, who demanded money in return for sparing the lives of him and his mother. He gave them all he had, but it wasn't enough, and they forced him to watch as they repeatedly raped his mother. Afterward, sick, wounded, shamed beyond reason and without a will to live, his mother could go no farther and she begged her son to end her life. He obeyed. He led her into a tent, told her to lie down and asked her to close her eyes. As she rested, he drove with the palm of his hand a sharpened nail through her eyeball and into her brain. The guilt and horror of that moment chilled his heart. He became impervious to feelings, and he trusted no one. In America, he earned money by collecting trash. Within ten years, he'd made a fortune by cornering the market for platinum in the days when you could do that kind of thing. Until he died, he spent his waking hours accumulating money.

Melanie's father married an actress, but the marriage ended when the actress committed suicide soon after Melanie was born. Melanie's father doted on his daughter, but his affection could not warm the chill in his heart or quell the screaming in his mind that kept him awake at night. To protect her from the same trauma as he'd endured, he imbued her with an appreciation for money. Not only would money help her to survive, it could also enhance her enjoyment of life.

At her father's hand, Melanie learned about the loneliness of a child whose parents have no love to give to their children. His emotions terrified him, and he had no vocabulary for love. He showed tenderness to other people using money, and he gave it freely to his daughter when she pleased him. When she didn't, he expressed his displeasure by withholding it. In his final gesture of extravagant emotion, he left his fortune to Melanie when he died. It didn't compensate for the absence of love in her heart or quell the suspicion with which she regarded the world, but it made her rich. And as her father said, "I've lived in places where you can't get rich. America is better."

Even if you lived in America, Melanie believed, like her father, that life was precarious. "When the bombs fall," her father told her, "and cities and highways and civilized order collapse, you will have to risk your life to cross the street for your monthly quart of milk. You will either stand in line with all the other timid, fearful sheep, or you will pay the bully who owns the cows. On your own, among the obedient sheep, you'll be lucky to get a sip of milk. If you want to live rather than merely survive, you will turn to the people who prosper without laws. You will turn to the thugs and the gangsters who will meet you at midnight in a dark alley to hand over a quart of milk. If you have the money, they will sell to you all the milk you want. But you need money."

Melanie relied on her wealth for the support and comfort that the rest of us find in other people. She could smother her fear in the fabric of a dress, clutch to her breast a pair of shoes and feel joy, wash away with alcohol and cocaine the despairing threat of her own vacant self-awareness, convince herself with diamonds and gold that she had value. She clung to anything that might give her the illusion of meaning in her life. She regarded other people as symptoms of disorder. They exhausted her. They performed no useful function. Like mosquitoes, their presence disoriented her and distracted her from her primary interest, which was herself. That's why Melanie retreated to her dressing room, where she could remove herself from the irritations of her life, gaze into the mirrored walls and surround herself with images of people just like her.

Usually she liked what she saw. But tonight, she'd observed that her mauve leather dress resembled the dress worn by Mary Louise and that it had flattered the teenager far more than her. With slashes from a tube of lipstick, Melanie had marked on the dress the flaws that she hadn't noticed earlier. When she'd finished marking the dress, she swallowed a mouthful of her champagne cocktail. Then she unfastened the dress, let it slide down her body to the floor and used the lipstick to highlight the flaws on herself. No matter which way she turned or how she held herself in the light, she felt much older than her age. So far, she'd resisted the lure of plastic surgery. She held in disdain the women who relied on plastic surgeons to disguise the telltale fingerprints of time. But now she felt herself relenting. She'd decided when the Season ended that she would contact a plastic surgeon in Manhattan and show him exactly what she wanted him to do.

She slouched in the chair. She'd drawn red crescents under her eyes, a red line on the flesh that sagged under her jawbone. She'd carved red slashes with the lipstick across her breasts, her abdomen and her thighs.

"I feel like a stranger in my own body," she said.

When Darius offered his hand, she took it and pulled herself to her feet. "I'm frightened," she said.

Melanie sang along to the recorded music. "You will start out standing, proud to steal her anything she sees."

The song reminded her of a way she wanted to be, long before her father had died. It captured the way Melanie had wanted her father to feel about her and, later, other men when they met her. She wanted a man to feel proud to know her. For her sake, he would abandon himself to his passion. He would steal for her, even kill for her. What woman doesn't want a man willing do that? But such a man has to be strong. Otherwise a woman feels no sense of triumph in bending him to her will. Melanie had never bent her father to her will. She never could. But she had his money and, at first, that was almost as good as his love.

Melanie pulled away from Darius, swallowed another mouthful of her cocktail and looked again in the mirror. Now she liked everything she saw. She'd grown up pretty, tried to become beautiful and, when that hadn't worked, succeeded in looking expensive. Money had paid for everything that she'd ever wanted. Only poor people believed that you could live happily without it. In a world of risk, money made her feel secure. It paid for her handbags and hobbies and servants. With each dollar she spent, she felt more authentic. The more she spent, the more credit she could take for the life that she created for herself and the less she had to attribute to luck or God or fate. Melanie left nothing to chance. Money allowed her that luxury, as well. She just wished that a man would sometimes see through all her money and cherish her for the woman she really was.

Wishing made Melanie feel vulnerable, and that made her angry. You weren't supposed to feel this way when you had everything you'd ever wanted. She began again to apply the lipstick. She ran it twice over her mouth, leaving a wider swath this time. She ran the lipstick down the side of her face and under her chin. She drew a red line across her throat. She smiled when she did that. She looked like a clown. She drew red circles around her breasts. The patterns on her flesh drew attention to her body. They made her feel significant. She understood why people got tattooed.

Melanie studied her reflection in the mirrored walls. She defined herself by the dimensions of her body. She was aware of more abstract dimensions, but she could not control them or manipulate them. It was all she could do to contain them. They weren't important, and she didn't trust them. No one appreciated those abstract dimensions anyway except perhaps Monsignor Klinzing at St. Edward.

"She never stumbles. She's got no place to fall," she sang. "The law can't touch her at all."

She watched Darius, saw him studying his own reflection in the mirrored walls. He had straight blonde hair, blue eyes and thin lips. His tanned skin seemed highly polished, like a porcelain doll's. At first glance, you could almost mistake him for a teenager until you noticed the hardness in his eyes and the meanness in the set of his mouth. He lifted his hand and ran his fingers across the image of his face. "Time for a facial," he said.

He leaned forward, caressed her shoulder, brushed his lips over her cheek and down her neck. Melanie sighed. "That's better," she said.

Melanie's skin felt like parchment, but Darius persevered. It was, after all, his job, and he did it well. Now he felt Melanie's hand through the fabric of his pants, pressing against the inside of his thigh. He breathed in the scent of her perfume as he ran the tip of his tongue past her ear. When he felt her hand cupping his genitals, he moved his hips. That, too, was part of his job. Darius delivered small kisses to the wrinkled flesh of Melanie's throat until he reached the arc of her breasts. It was like necking with a lizard.

Darius thought of the success he'd achieved in selling Mike's sculptures tonight at prices even higher than he'd anticipated. He was looking forward tonight to joining Mike in Kleppman's guesthouse. He liked Kleppman's parties. He liked the drugs, the abandonment to pleasure, the suspension of time that he felt when the young girls flattered him with their admiration and their kisses. He hoped that Mary Louise had invited girls as nubile and youthful as the ones she'd brought last time. He turned his attention back to Melanie. He led her slowly out of the closet. When he looked across the bedroom, he saw that Mike was gone.

Six

In limousines and rental cars, the girls arrived at the service gate of Kleppman's property on South Ocean Boulevard. It was after ten o'clock, but a groundskeeper stood in the shadows by the gate and directed them to the two-storey house secluded behind a landscaped knoll.

At the front steps, they fluttered like sparrows in groups of two or three before one of them opened the door, releasing a torrent of music that poured across the lawn toward the ocean.

Inside, some of the girls puffed on cigarettes with exaggerated nonchalance. Tall, large-breasted and willowy, they tottered on stiletto heels like novice ice skaters, surreptitiously tugging at their short skirts, halter tops and bodices. Most of them had been here before, but they still stared wide-eyed, like supplicants in the Vatican, at the opulence of the house.

In the foyer, under a crystal chandelier, Mary Louise met the girls and told them to select a gift from among the Prada handbags, Rolex watches, iPhones and Hermes scarves displayed on a walnut table. Each girl studied these objects as if they wouldn't just feed an appetite but enhance her capacity for love, as well. Mary Louise told them not to touch the lizard that Kleppman had positioned on the table. "It's a work of art," she said. "Very expensive. I know the artist."

In the living room, four men sat on deep-cushioned chairs and a couch upholstered in floral silk. The girls were much taller than the men, except for Hamilton Roebuck, who slouched in a chair with a highball glass of Scotch in his hand.

Four of the girls continued through the living room and down a hallway to the oak-paneled library. Bathed in light from discreet wall sconces, they removed their shoes and padded barefoot across the Isfahan carpet. Two of the girls joined Kleppman's Russian friend, Leonard Friesen, on a long leather couch. They tucked their tanned legs under themselves as he leaned back, spread his arms and pulled them against him. Facing them across a low wooden table, Oscar Hornbeam leaned back on an identical couch. Relieved to be free of his wife, whom he'd sent home, drunk, in an Uber, he'd already unbuttoned his silk shirt, and now he invited the other two girls to stroke his chest.

From a pantry behind a wall of first editions, Shirko, the juice-bar owner, brought drinks in Norlan whisky glasses and cocaine in small crystal dipping bowls, placing them on the table between the two couches. Shirko didn't bring plastic glasses to Kleppman's parties. Kleppman didn't allow plastic on his property.

As the night unfolded, Mary Louise climbed the spiral staircase to the master bedroom to lay out sheets and lotions on a massage table. With an app on her phone, she selected a playlist of music that included "Green Fields" by the Brothers Four. She went back downstairs to tell a girl named Celeste that Mister Kleppman was waiting for her. Celeste had been sitting on the lap of Doctor Cyrus Beltran and was wearing his Panama hat. "She's with me," he said. It was the first time that Mary Louise had seen Doctor Cyrus Beltran without his hat. He reminded her of the mailman in Lantana.

"Don't worry, Mister Beltran," said Mary Louise. "Marcia's coming. You'll like her, too."

"Doctor Beltran," he corrected her. "And Celeste is staying with me."

"Sorry, sweetheart," said Celeste. She replaced the hat on Beltran's head. "Maybe another night."

"We can't keep Mister Kleppman waiting," said Mary Louise.

At the foot of the staircase, Mary Louise handed Celeste two one-hundred-dollar bills. She stuffed them into her panties.

"If we do this every week," Celeste said, "we'll be rich."

Upstairs, Celeste found Keith Kleppman in the master bedroom wearing nothing but a small towel around his waist. A mat of grey hair covered his chest. The Brothers Four were singing, "Once there were green fields kissed by the sun."

Kleppman removed his towel and lay down on his back on the massage table. "Take off your clothes," he said.

Celeste stroked his chest while Kleppman held his penis in his hand. With his other hand, he reached into a rack attached to the frame of the bed and held up a vibrator. It hummed as he placed it against Celeste's crotch. "You like that, don't you, honey?" he said.

Downstairs in the library, Mary Louise instructed one of the two girls with Leonard Friesen to join Kleppman in the master bedroom and told Leonard that she'd send another girl to join him.

She walked with the first girl to the foot of the stairs. "He said Paco was going to use you in a shoot on Monday," said Mary Louise. "For Calvin Klein, I think."

"That's awesome," said the girl, swallowing the wine in her glass, her third of the evening.

"You have to be at the agency at eleven," Mary Louise said.

"I have a Spanish test on Monday," the girl said. "I'll say I'm sick, but I'll need a note."

"Have you got the bra and panties?" Mary Louise said. "He wants to see you in the bra and panties."

The girl went upstairs. She removed her clothes outside the door to the bedroom. Kleppman turned to look at her as she carried her wine glass toward him wearing a red brassiere and a pair of red silk boxer shorts monogrammed in gold thread with her initials. Celeste was still massaging Kleppman's chest and stomach.

"You've gained weight," he said, looking across the room as he guided Celeste's hand toward his genitals. "You'll need to do something about your hair before you meet Paco."

"Yes, sir," the girl said.

"Turn around," said Kleppman. "Show me your ass."

She turned around.

"Come over here," Kleppman said.

The girl said later that Kleppman made her feel uncomfortable. But she felt grateful for his gifts, his referral to a modeling agency and the money that he gave her. "I just close my eyes," she said, "and I think about the cash and I'm like, 'This is worth it'."

Like Mary Louise, the girls felt a mild thrill whenever they sensed that Kleppman and his friends were getting aroused. There was something satisfying about seducing a man as old as your father and watching him turn into a helpless boy with a hard-on.

In the library, Mary Louise joined Leonard Friesen on the couch. Leonard was holding the jeweled lizard. He said he'd offered to buy it that night from Kleppman and planned to add it to his art collection. "One hundred thousand dollar I pay it," he said.

"For your collection?" said Mary Louise.

"For lizard," said Leonard Friesen.

Mary Louise sat up.

"What's wrong?" said Leonard Friesen.

"That's a lot of money," she said.

Leonard Friesen waved his hand. "Is nothing," he said.

"I bought one for ten dollars," she said.

"A knock-off, must be," said Leonard Friesen.

As the night continued, Mary Louise and two other girls strolled in their panties through the house. Shirko was in the kitchen with the maid. Leonard Friesen and Oscar Hornbeam went upstairs with their girls, leaving the library deserted. The girls sat on the leather couches with their legs curled under them. Mary Louise activated a panel in the wall that slid back to reveal a TV so they could watch music videos. At one point, Doctor Cyrus Beltran wandered into the room wearing a silk robe, purple slippers and his indispensable hat. He stood beside one of the girls, letting his hand rest on her head as he watched a video by Grimes. The electronic music pulsed with the rhythm of a heartbeat. For almost a minute, no one in the room said a word. Finally, Cyrus Beltran removed his hand from the girl's head. "Fantastic," he said, and he walked out again.

On Kleppman's orders, the kitchen staff had laid China plates and silverware on a table in the dining room, although as one of the maids said later to the police, "Most of the guests wouldn't have cared if we'd set the table with gardening tools." Tonight, when one of the girls wandered into the kitchen, the maid offered to fetch her a plate of cold cuts and fruit, but the girl asked instead for a bowl of Cap'n Crunch with milk.

Around four in the morning, Mary Louise, still buzzing from the coke, went upstairs to lie on Kleppman's bed. Kleppman had disappeared into another room. She rested her head on her hand and looked at texts on her iPhone. She could hear music from downstairs, but she didn't hear the front door open or her friend Celeste walking outside in her bare feet.

Celeste was wearing a T-shirt with a picture of Mickey Mouse on the front and a pair of pink panties with two one-hundred-dollar bills tucked under the elastic. The sky was clear. The calm water of the lagoon reflected a sprinkling of stars. Weaving across the closely trimmed grass, Celeste stumbled onto the concrete dock where Kleppman moored his Aquariva Super. The concrete chilled her bare feet, so she reversed her direction, crossed the lawn and wobbled down the driveway to the service entrance that led onto South Ocean Boulevard. She wanted to look at the moon. When she reached the road, the asphalt beneath her feet felt so warm and inviting, she decided to lie down on her back to look up at the sky. She could hear the ocean hurling waves onto the beach. She was watching the stars and listening to the ocean when a black Maybach came silently along the road with its lights out. When the car ran over her, Celeste let out a squeal. And then she was dead. An hour later, the sun was rising over the edge of the ocean when a triathlete on a bicycle passed her body. Reluctant to interrupt his training regimen, he waited until he reached his destination in Manalapan before he called the police.

By the time the police came onto Kleppman's property, the girls had gone home. Kleppman's houseman had surveyed the living room and the library and picked up the sex toys that the guests had left on the floor. He was about to put them in the dishwasher when he saw the police outside. They apologized for disturbing the household at such an early hour. The houseman, who was loyal to Kleppman and earned a good income for doing his job, said there was no one in the house except a few staff. He said he didn't know where the dead girl had come from. His employer had held a party the previous night, he said, but she wasn't among the guests. The police said not to worry; they'd come back later to ask a few more routine questions. When they returned, the houseman said he'd contacted most of the guests who had attended the party, but no one recognized the girl. He also told them that someone had stolen the lizard. "I'm quite sure it wasn't one of the guests," he said. "None of Mister Kleppman's friends would do that." When the police told him that the owner of the sculpture should report the theft to his insurance company, Kleppman filed a claim for a hundred and fifty thousand dollars. If he hadn't done that, no one would have questioned the value of the sculpture, looked more closely at the identity of the artist who made it or discovered that he had a brother.

The following week, Kleppman told his houseman to send three dozen roses to Celeste's mother. Mary Louise gave him the address.

PART TWO

How many times have you heard someone say,
If I had his money, I'd do things my way?"
Jack Rhodes/Red Hayes

One

Dwayne Forbes had dreamed for years about living in the tropics, away from the Canadian winters, but for a long time he couldn't figure out how to get there. He was afraid of flying, and he couldn't afford to take a cruise. Until that day in March when he took the freeway exit ramp that led him to Palm Beach, he hadn't realized that he could get to the tropics by truck.

Dwayne Forbes grew up in Petrolia, a small town in Ontario near the border-crossing into Michigan. There used to be oil in Petrolia. Then there were refineries. Now there's a post office, a school, a gas station and a milk store, and a few hundred people who go somewhere else every day to work. Most of them feel deeply conflicted about money. All of them want more of it, but they regard with suspicion and envy anyone who has more of it than they do.

Unlike most people in town, Dwayne didn't want money. He regarded it with a loathing almost as pathological as the greed with which the rest of us pursue it. Unfortunately, we live in a time when people assess each other by their wealth. That's not such a bad thing. Money is a lot easier to acquire than a pedigree. It took a thousand years and a hundred revolutions before ordinary people like Keith Kleppman or Melanie Merriwether's father or you and I could acquire a fortune and all the privileges that go with it. These days, if you live in America, you can start a company like Amazon and make a million dollars in five years, and you don't have to kill anyone to do it.

Dwayne left Petrolia about a month after his twenty-fourth birthday. He quit his job working the night shift in a gas station by the highway, packed everything he owned, including his sculpting tools and a few of his pieces, into a Montreal Canadiens hockey bag, tossed it into the box of his Datsun pickup and drove across the Blue Water Bridge from Sarnia into Port Huron. He drove south for thirty-six hours, intending to go all the way to the

Gulf of Mexico, until he saw the sign for Palm Beach. As soon as he turned off the freeway he saw his first palm tree. He'd never seen one up close. He turned down a side street that led him into Lake Worth, where palm trees grow like weeds right on people's front lawns.

Driving through the town, he spotted a For Rent sign in front of a house on North K Street and decided he wanted to live there. He drove to a gas station and used a payphone to call the number on the sign. The landlord owned a car dealership on the Dixie Highway, about a mile from the house, and said Dwayne could have the place for three hundred dollars in cash to cover the first and last month's rent. He told Dwayne to drop by with the money. Dwayne had brought cash with him from Canada in a paper bag that he'd hidden under the spare tire of the pickup. "No problem," he said.

At this point in his journey, Dwayne hadn't shaved in a couple of days, but he was wearing a clean T-shirt and jeans. After he ran a comb through his fair hair and checked his reflection in the rearview mirror, he thought he looked all right: a big, good-natured bear of a man with an unassuming air about him that invited total strangers to ask him for directions.

"Where you from?" said the car dealer, who was used to renting his house to poor black families from Mississippi and Alabama.

"Canada," said Dwayne.

"Cold up there."

Since Dwayne had spent most of his American money on gas, cheeseburgers and maple fudge, he offered to pay his deposit with a handful of brown, wrinkled Canadian two-dollar bills, but the car dealer shook his head. "That money's no good here," he said.

It took Dwayne two days to exchange his money, because he didn't have a bank account or a credit card. Fortunately, the car dealer let him park the Datsun behind the service garage. At night, he slept in the truck with the doors locked. During the day, he drove from one bank to another and also looked for a job. In the evenings, he sat on the tailgate of his truck and worked on a block of wood with his carving tools. It was something that he'd learned to do as a boy on bus trips to hockey games. His teammates ate sunflower seeds and spit the shells on the floor as they looked out the window at the snow-covered bean fields between Petrolia and the surrounding towns like Chatham, Woodstock and Strathroy. Dwayne was allergic to nuts. One taste, and his throat constricted and his face buzzed with a current like an electric blanket. He didn't know if he was allergic to sunflower seeds, but he didn't want to take a chance. Instead, he distracted himself on these road trips by carving figures out of broken hockey sticks with his pocketknife. At the end of a trip, the floor under the seat that he shared with a teammate crackled with wood chips and seed hulls.

In the ninth grade, an art teacher at the high school in Petrolia noticed Dwayne's passion and gave him two books, one about a Romanian sculptor named Constantin Brancusi, the other about Alberto Giacometti. Dwayne studied the photographs in these books with the same intensity as his team-mates studied photographs of hockey players. To the roots of his being, he absorbed the beauty of Spoon Woman, l'Homme qui marche 1, Bird in Space, and then he began to imitate works that he saw in the photographs until he could do with a folding knife what Brancusi did with sculpting tools. When he finished a carving, he polished it with beeswax on a rag torn from an old T-shirt until the grain of the wood emerged like the patterns on the wing of a butterfly. He became good enough at imitating the images in the book that you would have had trouble telling the difference between a Brancusi and a Dwayne Forbes, except by the quality of the wood.

In his high-school art classes, Dwayne had daydreamed occasionally of becoming an artist, although he wasn't sure what the word meant. It had something to do with fame. Giacometti, Brancusi, and all the other artists he'd heard about were famous, although their fame seemed secondary to their achievements, and there were many other famous people who had achieved nothing at all. Most of the famous artists he liked were dead. Dwayne had no interest in paying such a high price to attract attention to himself or his carvings. He also sensed that art had something to do with honesty, humility and courage, but he didn't really know why except that, whenever he worked on a sculpture, it took all his strength to overcome the deep-seated suspicion that it was a pointless exercise that would amount to nothing. He felt the same way when he went to work at the gas station in Petrolia. Most of the time he didn't think about himself as an artist or anything other than who he was: a kid who liked to fart around with wood when he wasn't busy getting on with his life and plotting a future when he could leave home.

At home on Oozloffsky Street, Dwayne's stepfather made fun of him, told him he was a freak, a pansy, a moron and a weakling who couldn't even eat nuts without breaking out in a rash. He said Dwayne reminded him of an old man. All he needed, he said, was a corncob pipe and a rocking chair, and he could whittle his days away while his beard grew down to his chest. His mother said Dwayne reminded her of her first husband, Dwayne's father, a dreamer and a ne'er do well whom she hated for deserting her by dying and leaving her with a son like him. She never encouraged Dwayne and could hardly look at the sculptures that he made. If he left a half-finished carving on the kitchen table, she'd throw it away, so Dwayne moved to the basement where his mother and stepfather wouldn't bother him.

Before Dwayne left school for good, the same art teacher gave him a set of Japanese wood-carving tools. Who knows where she got them in a town like Petrolia? Dwayne hid them in a crawl space at home behind the oil tank in the basement and never told anyone about them.

Dwayne spent hours on end using his tools to coax figures from pieces of wood. He discovered that they revealed themselves only if he allowed them to emerge on their own terms. He learned never to force his will onto a piece of wood, never to grow impatient, but to remain attentive and obedient to its integrity. He could sense the spirit within wood, and he learned to seduce it into the light of the world. As he removed one delicate layer after another, he felt as if he was earning the trust of a lover.

Eventually people would hover over his sculptures, spellbound by their mystical simplicity. Like his heroes, Dwayne Forbes would become famous, and his work would sell for prices that he never could have imagined. But that was much later, and Dwayne would never know the value that the world placed on his work, nor would he have cared.

In Lake Worth, Dwayne slept behind the car dealership for two days until he finally found a currency exchange in West Palm Beach that took the Canadian bills off his hands in return for an eighteen-per-cent commission. He ended up with about five hundred American dollars and some coins. But he figured it all worked out for the better, because he got the house of his dreams and a job, too.

The house on North K Street had everything he wanted: a kitchen, a bathroom, a living room and a bedroom, one front window, a slanted roof and a parking pad. His neighbors' houses were the color of Listerine and cantaloupe, but his house was pink, like candy floss. In front of some of the houses, stunted palm trees had shed big slabs of bark that lay on the ground like side panels from a car. But nothing grew in front of Dwayne's house except some wild grass. The blades of grass grew no higher than his ankles, so he would never have to mow the lawn. But they were as tough as a shredded Pepsi jug and could slice through flesh. After he moved into the place, he seldom walked across the yard, even in his work boots.

Dwayne landed the job when he got stuck one afternoon in a traffic jam on the Federal Highway near Boynton Beach. A construction crew was reinforcing a bridge. While he sat in the pickup, he struck up a conversation with one of the workers and discovered that the crew boss had just fired the flagman. The flagman had come to work that morning after spending the previous night in a bar and neglected to raise his hand-held Stop sign to keep traffic from traveling north across the single open lane of the bridge. A woman driving north with her two children and their dog from Fort Lauderdale had driven straight into a southbound dump truck. She wasn't going very fast, and no one was hurt, but the dog ran away, and the truck spilled its load of mud and sea-weed onto the road and shut down the bridge completely. The resulting traffic jam was Dwayne's good fortune.

Dwayne found the foreman and told him he needed a job. The foreman, a tall, middle-aged man with a grey ponytail, liked Canadi-ans and agreed to pay Dwayne in cash. He said he could start immedi-ately. Dwayne promised that he wouldn't screw up. For the next four months, he didn't miss a day or arrive even a minute late. With the mon-ey he earned, he bought a second-hand bed, some furniture and cutlery. When the job was finished, the foreman asked Dwayne if he wanted to keep working for him, but the next project was in Clarksville, Texas, and Dwayne wanted to stay a little longer in his pink house and enjoy the palm trees in Lake Worth, so he turned down the offer.

Without a job, Dwayne started his day by walking three blocks to the Dunkin Donuts shop, where he picked up a discarded copy of the Palm Beach Daily Post from a shelf inside the front door and spent a few minutes looking through the help-wanted ads. He ignored the ones that invited people to work on commission as telephone solicitors or sales reps for vacuum cleaners, even if they promised an income of $1,000 A WEEK! Dwayne knew that people worked hard for their money, and he didn't feel comfortable asking them to spend it on something that they probably didn't need. He also ignored the ads for drivers, because he still had a Canadian license. But when he saw an ad for a job that he could do, like a swimming-pool installer or construction worker, he called the employer on a disposable cell phone that he bought for six dollars at Wal-Mart. Sometimes the person who answered the phone asked him a few questions about his experience and his skills and then said he wasn't suitable for the job. Other times, the job was already taken. Once in a while, he was asked to leave his number. He couldn't take calls on his cellphone, so he gave out the number of his landlord's car dealership. So far it hadn't inconvenienced his landlord, because no one had called him back.

Dwayne didn't feel hopeful when he answered want ads. He made a better impression on people if they saw him in person. He walked around his neighborhood a few times, stopping at machine shops and small factories on streets near the highway to ask for work. He figured he'd save money if he could walk to work, and he wouldn't have to worry about traffic. But so far, he'd had no luck with want ads or personal visits. Now he planned to go farther afield. He started driving every day to nearby industrial parks, starting with the ones near the airport. Sooner or later, he knew he'd find something.

When he wasn't looking for a job, Dwayne explored his neighborhood, gathering scraps of wood from trash bins and vacant lots. With his Japanese carving tools that he'd brought from Petrolia, he transformed the wood into abstract figures of lizards like the ones he'd seen in the parks beside Lake Worth. He polished these figures with lemon oil and beeswax and positioned them under the windowsills of his house, out of the sunlight. A smaller piece took him about two weeks. A larger one could take a month or more.

On a Sunday morning during one of his walks around Lake Worth, Dwayne passed a small house that had been converted into a church called the Bautiste Eglise. His mother had taken him and his brother, Mike, to Sunday school a few times after she'd joined the Jehovah's Witnesses. In hindsight, Dwayne didn't think she believed any of the religious claptrap; she just wanted to go swimming with the children in the summer, and the Witnesses operated a camp outside of Petrolia beside a lake with a supervised beach. But Dwayne liked the way he felt in church and every so often he attended a service. On this day, when he went inside the Bautiste Eglise, he discovered that everyone there spoke French. Although he'd studied French in high school, Dwayne didn't understand a word they said, but he enjoyed the music and he didn't think God cared if he prayed in French, English or any other language. In the midst of the small congregation he stood beside a skinny little man wearing a brown suit and a straw hat that looked as if he'd sat on it. The man turned to Dwayne and stared at him through thick glasses with black plastic rims until Dwayne pointed to himself and said, "Canada." The black man nodded and said, "IET."

After church, Dwayne pulled a Montreal Canadiens hockey jersey over his head and took his sculptures in a pillowcase to a flea market that he'd passed several times in a strip-mall parking lot on the Dixie Highway. Other vendors there did a booming business selling kerchiefs, scarves, salad bowls, table lamps made from wine bottles, Confederate flags, stuffed turtles, velvet paintings of Michael Jackson and Princess Diana and cancelled boarding passes from exotic airlines. Once in a while, a visitor stopped to chat with Dwayne. A man in a leather hat offered to buy his Montreal Canadiens jersey. Most of the time, he sat on the tailgate of the Datsun, drank coffee and watched the people who wandered through the market.

On this day, towards the end of the afternoon, a purple Aston Martin with tinted windows pulled into the strip-mall parking lot. The car's body throbbed with the pulsing bass of a rap song. The driver turned off the car and climbed out. He was short, dressed in a pink jacket over a red T-shirt and blue jeans that had been ironed, with a crease as sharp as a knife blade. He wore aviator sunglasses and a baseball cap, similar to Dwayne's, but ten times more expensive because it came from Dolce & Gabbana.

He moved to the passenger door and held it open for a woman who unfolded herself from the front seat until she towered over the man. She minced her way to the front of the car, adjusting her breasts under her orange halter top. She was wearing tight white jeans and red sandals with stacked heels. Long orange earrings dangled amidst her tangled mane of blonde hair. Her toenails were painted the same shade of orange.

"Gimme a hand," a voice called from the car.

The man hustled back to the passenger door to help another woman step onto the pavement. Her companions walked ahead of her straight past Dwayne, but this one stopped to admire one of his sculptures. She had several diamond studs in her left ear and a large gold hoop in her right ear. She wore black cowboy boots, black tights with holes ripped in the legs and a black T-shirt that stopped above a gold navel ring. The T-shirt displayed the word SUCK in bold white letters over her breasts. Her black hair was tied back tightly above her head.

"I'll catch up," she said as her companions walked away toward a display of jewellery and blouses.

"You make this?" she said to Dwayne. She was lissome and shapely, like a young sapling. She reminded him of a little girl masquerading as an adult woman.

"I did," he said.

"How much?" she said.

"I have a hard time putting a price on my work," Dwayne said.

"It has to be worth something," she said.

Dwayne looked into her blue eyes. He told me later that they reminded him of a Hockney swimming pool that promised to embrace him in fantastic delights. "How much is your beauty worth?" he said, surprising himself with his boldness

The girl blushed then quickly hid her embarrassment behind a cloud of suspicious hostility.

"Get lost," she said, and she started to walk away.

"Sorry," said Dwayne. "I didn't mean to upset you."

The tone of his voice must have reassured the girl. She came back to the truck and picked up the sculpture. She loved lizards, she said. "Lizards are weird," she said. "Some people think I'm weird. I've always wanted a tattoo of a lizard. I'd have to get it where daddy couldn't see it. I've already got one tattoo. Want to see it?"

She turned her head and lifted her hair to reveal a sprig of sinuous green ivy tattooed up the back of her neck. It reminded Dwayne of a Burne-Jones painting he'd seen at an art gallery in Toronto. "You can't see it if I let my hair down," she said, letting her hair down.

The girl said her name was Mary Louise. Dwayne noticed a tiny gold stud in her nose.

Dwayne said he lived a few blocks away, on North K Street. The girl said her father was the pastor at the Church of the Lord Jesus on Johnson Street, not far from Dwayne's house. In the Church of the Lord Jesus, she said, lizards are sacred.

Dwayne said he'd gone that morning to the Bautiste Eglise, where everyone in the congregation was from Haiti and spoke French. Mary Louise said he should come to her father's church. Her father conducted his services in English, she said. Then she bought one of Dwayne's sculptures, for ten dollars.

"My friend," she said, nodding toward her companions, "sells weird shit like this."

"That's great," said Dwayne.

"He's got a gallery and everything," she said. "In Palm Beach."

"No kidding," said Dwayne.

"It's called M2," she said.

Dwayne looked at Mary Louise's earrings and the jewel in her bellybutton. What did she know about art? But it was the first sculpture that he'd sold in two months. Maybe his luck was changing.

"He knows a lot of artists," she said. "Rollo Barnes. You know him?"

Dwayne shook his head. "No," he said.

Clutching the sculpture, Mary Louise looked around for her friends. When she spotted them, she started to move away, but then she hesitated. "You should come to my father's church," she said. She looked into his eyes and smiled. "Visit your lizard."

Dwayne wondered if she was pulling his leg, but she held his gaze, and all he could see was that promise.

"I'll do that," he said. "Mary Louise."

"See you around," she said. "Dwayne."

She rejoined her friends then to wander through the market but returned a half hour later to introduce them. The tall blonde girl with the orange top she introduced as Celeste. The man in the pink jacket was Darius. "He owns the gallery," she said. "M2?"

"I like your work," said Darius.

"Thanks," said Dwayne.

Mary Louise held up her sculpture. "I do too," she said.

"What do you know about art?" said Celeste.

"More than you," said Mary Louise.

Darius handed Dwayne a business card. "Drop by sometime," he said.

"Sure," said Dwayne, "I'll do that." But Darius had already turned away to walk with the girls toward his purple Aston Martin.

Dwayne knew that people often extended empty invitations. He wasn't sure if they did it to make themselves look good or because they couldn't think of anything else to say. He looked at the card, noted the name, Darius Pierre, and the address on Worth Avenue, then put the card in his pocket.

Two

If Dwayne had traveled about a mile across the inland lake to Palm Beach, he could have taken his sculptures to the M2 Gallery and sold them for far more than ten dollars. With the money he made, he could have spent more time on his sculpting and less time looking for a job to support himself. But Dwayne had never expected to make much money from his art. When someone gave him ten dollars for one of his lizards, he felt as if he was accepting a tip for good service, and then he looked for someone else who might need it more than he did.

Under his mother's Christian influence, reinforced by his art teacher's admiration for unyielding artists who refuse to sacrifice the clarity of their vision on the altar of commerce, Dwayne had grown up with a crippling aversion to money. In Dwayne's estimation, greed, like gluttony, was a sin, and excessive wealth, like obesity, was the price you paid for indulging it. By the same measure, he regarded the opulence and extravagance of wealth as a testament to corruption and self-indulgence. Ostentation embarrassed him. He wanted to turn away from it, the way he felt when he stood beside couples making out at bus stops. Clueless about economic theory, he suspected that a dollar acquired by a rich man deprived a poor man of the same amount and that poverty would end if rich people gave up their wealth. In his eyes, poor people were endowed by definition with virtue, as if the absence of money reflected the absence of avarice.

He sensed the relationship between imagination, freedom and infinity, and he knew that life had far more to offer than the satisfaction of an appetite. Convinced that people who abandon themselves to their appetites must feel profoundly lonely, he felt pity for the wealthy, in the same way as he felt sorry for a fat person who couldn't stop eating. Pity allowed him to feel virtuous. Feeling pity, he didn't have to question his own shortcomings.

Rather than questioning his opinions, he reinforced them with random quotations, aphorisms and observations like a lawyer marshaling evidence to win his case. He believed that money was the root of all evil, all that glitters is not gold, and the best things in life are free. He believed that his favorite sport of hockey had been corrupted by money and that money had corrupted his favorite team, the Montreal Canadiens, into the athletic equivalent of a Potemkin village whose familiar appearance belied the absence of its soul. On a piece of paper that he kept folded in his wallet, he'd written the words of the American painter George Catlin, who had lived for five years among the Arikara, Osage, Sioux, Omaha, Caddo, Wichita, Comanche and many other native tribes before they disappeared after the 1830s under the relentless pressure of Europe's genocidal invasion: "How I love a people who don't live for the love of money."

I don't see the world from Dwayne's perspective. His stubborn refusal to capitulate to the imperatives of commerce seemed quixotic and a waste of energy. In my world, survival depends on my ability to make a living. I can do that only if I earn money, and the more, the better. From the moment my mother gave birth to me, I've had to adapt to the world as it is, just as I would have adapted if I'd found myself in a jungle in Peru. Perhaps if the survival of my tribe depended on my ability to use a bow and arrow from the back of a horse to bring down a buffalo, I might have shared Dwayne's aversion to money. But I find greed far more interesting and more human than nostalgia or martyrdom to an antisocial dogma. The aspiring saints who bind themselves and flagellate their flesh to punish themselves for being human seem more threatening to my security and comfort than the libertines and rounders who indulge their desires and could care less if you or I followed their descent into the disco inferno. Wasn't Adolf Hitler the vegetarian who banned smoking?

Of course, Dwayne could afford to transform poverty into a virtue. He'd grown up in poverty and had become accustomed to its challenges and paltry rewards. He was young, male, white and single. He had no kids, no wife and no one but himself to look after. For a while, he didn't even have a girlfriend. Fortunately, his half-brother showed up to challenge Dwayne's ascetic fantasies.

Dwayne still hadn't found a job when Mike Rondell arrived in a cab on a Friday evening with all his worldly possessions in a battered suitcase. He said he'd been released at the end of the previous year from Archambault Prison, near Montreal, where he'd done time for fraud and possession with intent to distribute. He'd negotiated a shorter sentence by informing on the dealer who'd supplied him with cocaine. After his release, he went to work in Montreal, first as a roofer, then as a bouncer at Club Supersexe until he heard from his mother that Dwayne had gone to Florida and decided to join him.

On the night that Mike arrived, the temperature had fallen, as it does sometimes during the winter in Florida, to the low thirties. Frost had formed on the mewly grass like mold on cheese. To keep himself warm, Dwayne answered the door wearing a green nylon jacket that he'd won in a raffle for a junior hockey team called the Sarnia Sting, zipped to the collar.

Mike dropped his duffle bag and said, "As soon as I heard you was in Palm Beach, I says I have to come see this place for myself." Then he reached out and embraced Dwayne in a bear hug.

Dwayne's emotional antennae began to quiver. Mike would never have traveled so far just to visit him.

"This isn't Palm Beach," Dwayne said. "It's Lake Worth."

"Close enough," Mike said. He stood back to examine Dwayne's jacket. His eyes were the color and depth of steel. He had dark, greasy hair, sunken cheeks and a sallow complexion. A scar ran down the side of his neck from his ear and disappeared under the collar of his shirt. "Haven't seen one of those jackets for a while," he said.

"How'd you get across the border?" Dwayne said.

Mike said he'd ridden with a fake passport as far as Burlington, Vermont. From there, he'd hitchhiked down the coast, although Dwayne suspected that he'd probably stolen at least one car along the way. Dwayne didn't challenge his brother's story. He just wished Mike had told him that he was coming. His brother said it was Dwayne's fault.

"I would've called," Mike said, "if you had a fucking phone."

Dwayne stood in the doorway. He was wider and taller than his younger brother and outweighed him by about thirty pounds. But his size had never mattered much in a confrontation with Mike. Dwayne fought with reluctance, as a last resort. Mike fought willingly, to cause pain.

"You gonna invite me in or what?" Mike said, exhaling puffs of vapor into the cold air.

The house wasn't built for cold weather. It had no basement, no furnace, no fireplace, no storm windows and no heaters. It had no insulation in the walls or in the crawl space under the roof. When the wind blew, it rattled the windows.

"Like a goddam freezer," Mike said when Dwayne finally stepped aside.

Mike hadn't brought much with him in his sports bag, just a laptop computer, a few T-shirts and a couple of pairs of shorts, a black silk shirt, a pair of tailor-made black wool pants and black loafers made of leather as soft as butter. The shoes looked expensive. Dwayne figured he'd stolen them, probably from the car he'd stolen to get here. Mike hung the shirt and pants on a wire hanger in the little closet inside the front door. Dwayne looked at the fancy clothes and asked him if he intended to get a job as a waiter. His brother laughed. "I came to get rich," he said.

"I figured you had a reason for coming," said Dwayne.

"And to see you," said Mike. "That's what brothers are for."

Dwayne said his brother could stay with him for a few days. "But then you have to move on." He went outside to the truck and returned with a canvas tarpaulin, which he unrolled across the floor of the front room. "You can sleep on this," he said.

He handed his brother a pair of coveralls and then went to his room and closed the door. But almost as soon as he went to sleep, he opened his eyes again and saw Mike standing over the bed, shivering.

Mike had taken off all his clothes, removed his false front teeth so he wouldn't swallow them and draped the tarpaulin over his naked shoulders like Captain America. With his clothes off and his teeth out, he looked like an emaciated bald cat, coiled and ready to pounce.

"I've slept in tents warmer than this house," he said, sibilants whistling through the gap in his teeth.

"This won't last," said Dwayne.

Mike marched back to the front room. He gathered the tarpaulin more tightly around his shoulders and ducked his head to look out the window, as if he hoped to see an approaching heat wave rolling up the deserted street. He could have looked through the window without ducking, but Mike liked to act as if he was taller than he really was.

"Ask me," he said, "it's global warming. You don't fuck with Mother Nature."

"Cold spell is all," Dwayne said. "Happens every few years. So I hear."

Mike said they should get in the truck, turn on the heater and drive over to Palm Beach. "We can check out the big houses," he said.

"It's three o'clock in the morning, Mike," said Dwayne.

"Got something better to do?" said Mike.

Wide awake now and figuring that his brother might feel more motivated to earn a living if he saw what money could buy, Dwayne went back to his bedroom and got dressed. He remembered calculating once that he'd have to work for about thirty years to pay for a three-bedroom house in Petrolia. He had no idea how much a mansion in Palm Beach cost, but he figured he'd have to work for a light year to buy one. In the time it took to make that much money, he could travel to the moon on a bicycle, so he didn't even think about it. When he returned to the front room, Mike had put on his black shirt and black dress pants.

"Gonna do some business?" Dwayne said.

"You never know," Mike said. He rolled down the sleeves of his shirt to hide his tattoos and fastened the cuff buttons.

"Want your teeth?" said Dwayne.

"Fuck 'em," said Mike. "They hurt my gums."

Dwayne drove the Datsun across the bridge, followed the coast up South Ocean Boulevard past Sloans Curve and Mar-a-Lago, all the way to Barton Avenue, where the road curves inland, then cruised through the side streets of Palm Beach. Mike hardly noticed the ocean that pounded onto the shore or the first rays of the dawn sun glowing on the horizon, but the houses caught his attention. The more he looked at them, the more excited he became.

"Jesus Christ on a crutch," he said, "Will you look at the size of that fucking place. What would you give to live there?"

"You could buy a house like that someday," said Dwayne. "You just need a job."

Mike shifted in his seat to peer beyond a pair of stone elephants that stood like sentries at the entrance to a driveway. "You don't buy a place like that flipping burgers," he said.

"Who needs such a big house?" said Dwayne.

"You wouldn't understand," said Mike. "People expect more of you when you're good looking."

Dwayne glanced at his brother to see if he was joking. "The trouble with you, Mike, you think money's the answer to all your problems."

"I'd like to find out," Mike said. "Wouldn't you?"

"My problems, money wouldn't help."

"What problems do you have?" said Mike.

According to his brother, Dwayne had been lucky all his life. For one thing, he was older. That gave him a head start, Mike said. Also, Dwayne wasn't especially handsome, Mike said, didn't care about his appearance and dressed like a slob. Mike had always been the better-looking one. He was tall, black-haired and muscular, with dark eyes, a prominent jaw and a chiseled body like a sprinter. In the summer, he never worried the way Dwayne did about taking off his shirt. His skin tanned to the shade of a copper penny. Dwayne was self-conscious about his body. He thought he resembled a Smurf. His fair skin burned to the color of a red pepper in the sunlight, and he looked unhealthy. Doctors wondered about his blood pressure, checked for diabetes, advised him never to go outside in the sunshine unless he wore a long-sleeved shirt, a hat and enough sunscreen to baste a turkey.

In school, Mike was the whiz kid, Dwayne was the slow one, the doofus, the dim-wit who hid himself at the back of the class. Mike had skipped a grade in the same year as Dwayne had failed, and they'd ended up in the same class even though Dwayne was older. Dwayne spent most of his time that year alone, in the basement, whittling sticks. Even then, Mike seemed envious of him. But then, Mike had never felt satisfied. He'd always felt short-changed, as if fate had dealt him a bad hand in the poker game of life. Maybe, Dwayne thought, he placed unreasonably high expectations on himself and took no pride the way Dwayne did in his accomplishments, whatever they were.

Mike might have had all the advantages that a person could ask for: good looks, good health and intelligence. But those advantages had come without effort. When he wanted more and realized that he'd have to work for it, he'd been defeated by his own ambition. He grew lazy and used his intelligence to cut corners and play the angles. Dwayne remembered when Mike stole the bicycle that Dwayne had bought with money from his paper route. He sold it for thirty dollars and gave Dwayne five. With another three dollars, Mike bought a bouquet of flowers for their mother, and he kept the rest for himself. When Dwayne complained that Mike had stolen his bike, their mother told him that he should try harder to share things with his brother instead of keeping everything for himself. Dwayne didn't bother telling his stepfather. He knew what that prick would say.

Still, Dwayne admitted that he'd been lucky. How else could he explain his life? He could never have planned it this way. Here he was, living in a pink house in Florida on a street lined with palm trees. He'd earned enough money in the last few months to keep himself going until he could find another job.

"I have no problems," Dwayne said now as they turned at the end of Banyan Road. "My life's a bowl of fucking cherries."

"You know what else I like about this place?" said Mike.

"What?" said Dwayne.

"No bus stops."

"So?"

"Who can afford to live in a neighborhood, no one takes the bus?" Mike said. "Must be nice, eh."

As they returned home along the coast, a police car drove up behind the Datsun, flashed its lights and signaled to Dwayne to pull over. "Tell him to fuck off," Mike said.

"Got it," said Dwayne.

The policeman walked up to the driver's window and asked for Dwayne's license and registration. "Canada," he said when he looked at the documents. "I have a cousin in Nova Scotia."

"Nithe plathe," said Mike. Without his dental plate, he lisped when he raised his voice.

"Either one of you boys have an I.D. card?" said the cop.

"No, sir," said Dwayne. "What's that?"

"You get one at the station," said the cop. "Saves time, situations like this. That's if you plan to work here. Maybe not if you're Canadian."

"I have a summer home in Chester," said Mike.

"Never been there," said the policeman.

"Nova Scotia," said Mike. "Figured you might know it."

The cop looked again at Mike, then at Dwayne, returned the papers to Dwayne, told them to have a nice day and stay out of trouble. Dwayne let out a deep breath. He could feel drops of sweat rolling down his back.

"Shoulda told the athhole to fuck off," said Mike.

"A summer home in Chester?" Dwayne said.

"Shoulda said Monte Carlo."

"Fuck, Mike. You could charm the pants off Mother Teresa."

Mike stared out the window. As they approached the bridge to Lake Worth, he became agitated, bouncing his heel up and down on the floorboard with the insistent rhythm of a woodpecker's head against a tree. "I gotta tell you, man," he said. "This place is inspiring. It's time I stopped being an idiot. Fuck."

"We all make mistakes," said Dwayne, thinking his brother was re-examining the errors of his life.

"I just need a plan," said Mike, nodding his head.

"A man needs a goal," Dwayne said.

"A couple of breaks," Mike said.

"A steady job," said Dwayne.

His brother rolled down the window and spat into the street. "Fuck the job, Dwayne. You get a fucking job. I gotta think outside the box."

"I suppose," said Dwayne.

"You don't understand. Me, I gotta think like an artist."

"They teach you that in prison?" Dwayne said.

"That's what I know, bro," said Mike.

Dwayne had heard all this before. Mike was always hatching schemes to make a fortune, and he always had a plan for spending it, too. He seemed to think that, if he talked about money all the time, he'd eventually get some.

At first glance, his schemes seemed convincing, like the face of a fake Rolex watch. He'd once planned to import a stolen container-load of coffee beans from Brazil. Another time, he planned to ship a ton of gold bars embezzled from the Indonesian treasury to a refinery in Germany. With a crooked general in the Venezuelan army, he planned to obtain the concession to a mine in the jungle that produced a thousand ounces of gold a day or a month or a year, Dwayne couldn't remember exactly. A contact in Italy said he'd put Mike in touch with a factory that made counterfeit designer handbags. To get his half-assed plans off the ground, Mike just needed enough money to meet face-to-face with the business partner who would put the scheme into action. Since he never had any money of his own, he borrowed it, usually from Dwayne, always with the promise of repayment and bigger money to come.

On his trips to the world's centers of corruption, Mike sometimes succeeded in meeting the shiftless gangsters, bent generals and larcenous manufacturers of designer accessories who could put his get-rich-quick plan into action. But something always happened at the last minute that blew the plan apart. The container full of coffee beans fell off the ship into the Gulf of Mexico. The Indonesian treasurer tumbled out of an airplane into the jungles of Sumatra. The general fled Venezuela for an unknown destination. The handbag manufacturer's plant was raided by Interpol. When this happened, Mike seemed genuinely disappointed, and Dwayne felt disappointed, too, until he remembered that Mike had traveled to Rio de Janeiro, Jakarta, Caracas or Milan, places where Dwayne had never been, on money that Dwayne had earned by going to work every day. Then Dwayne just felt angry at himself that he'd fallen once again for one of Mike's schemes. He admired his brother's enthusiasm and he appreciated his generous intentions. There was even a chance that Mike could pull off one of his schemes. But it irked him that Mike couldn't afford a bus ticket but always kept his passport up to date. After the last aborted plan, Dwayne concluded that his brother was a no-hoper. He was like a kid who thought he could become a rock star by growing his hair, dressing up in a satin shirt and holding an untuned guitar.

"The trouble with you, Mike," Dwayne said, "you don't know the difference between a plan and a fantasy."

"I'll bet they say that to every man who dreams big," said Mike.

"What do you dream about, Mike?"

Mike thought for a moment as they drove up North K Street. "First, I'll get a new set of teeth," he said. "And then I'll hire someone to answer my phone."

Three

When he woke up later that morning, Dwayne found his brother pacing around the front room. Mike picked up one of the wooden lizards from the windowsill. "You still carving these things?" he said.

"It's what I do," said Dwayne.

"What do you do with 'em?"

"Take them to the flea market," said Dwayne. "Every Sunday."

"Sold any?" Mike said.

"One or two," Dwayne said.

"How much you sell them for?"

"Whatever someone wants to pay. Few weeks ago, a woman gave me ten bucks. Sometimes I get twenty for the big ones."

"You gonna make more?" Mike said. He picked up another figure.

"Probably," said Dwayne. "I have that log on the lawn."

Dwayne said he'd driven a few nights earlier with his chainsaw into the Everglades to look for firewood. When he got as far as the Okaloacoochee Slough, about two hours west of Lake Worth, he drove around the state park until he found a fallen tree. He'd used the chainsaw to cut a length of wood from the trunk. "Mahogany," he said. "Weighs a ton."

Mike asked him why he needed firewood. "You don't have a fireplace," he said.

Dwayne said he was going to burn it in the oven.

"Good way to die," said Mike.

"Keep the pipes from freezing," said Dwayne.

"Why not just burn one of your lizards?" Mike said.

"I'm not going to burn my carvings," Dwayne said.

"They're probably not worth shit."

"You never know."

"Trust me," Mike said. "I know. Besides," he said. "Who'd buy a work of art by a guy named Dwayne?"

Mike set the figure back on the windowsill and picked up a business card. "Who's Darius Pierre?" he said.

"Some guy," said Dwayne. "Runs a gallery in Palm Beach."

"M2 it says here," said Mike.

"He came to the flea market once," said Dwayne. "With that woman, bought one of my lizards."

"Guy gives you his card, he thinks you'll get in touch."

"It was just talk," said Dwayne.

"You should go see the guy."

"I don't know. It's a different world over there."

"Yeah," said Mike. "Like, it's fucking warm."

He pulled the tarpaulin over his shoulders and took his laptop computer into the kitchen. Dwayne said he was going fishing.

Four

Dwayne didn't actually fish. He thought fishing was as interesting as throwing stones at a tree. But he liked to walk over to Flagler Drive on Saturday mornings and watch other people fishing. It felt peaceful. He could let his thoughts wander as he sat in the sunshine and gazed across the water. The same guys came there every weekend with long poles and metal bait buckets to fish for bream. On the other side of the lake, lush green foliage seemed to swarm over the white walls and red rooftops of the Palm Beach mansions. Dwayne figured he could get a job over there as a gardener, but one of the fishermen told him that most gardeners in Palm Beach were Mexican.

Dwayne still hadn't found a job when he sat down that Saturday morning and watched a pelican gliding over the surface of the lake. The bird dipped its wingtip to stutter across the water like a kid running his fingers across the slats of a picket fence. On the far side soundless cars moved along South Ocean Boulevard past a house visible only by its roof looming above the trees. A black fisherman told Dwayne that Rod Stewart, the singer, owned the house. Whenever Dwayne heard the name of Rod Stewart, he remembered his mother sitting on a shabby couch in their house in Petrolia holding a half-empty glass of wine, listening to Rod Stewart singing a song called "Reason to Believe." She and Howard, his stepfather, had had a fight, and she was sad again. "If I had money I'd buy new clothes," he remembered her saying. "But I don't have money. How can I save money? I spend it all on you." Now as he looked across Lake Worth, the sappy Rod Stewart song drifted again through his mind like a vapor. "And see that big flag?" the fisherman said. "That there's Mister Trump's place. The President. That one over there belongs to Keith Kleppman." When the fisherman saw that the name didn't make an impression on Dwayne, he said, "Just another rich guy."

A jet rose over the houses and into the clouds. By the time the sound of its engines reached Dwayne, it had disappeared. The man said President Trump had sued the airport, trying to prevent planes from flying over his house. Dwayne sympathized with the President's concerns. It bothered him when noisy cars drove down North K Street, especially late at night when he was trying to sleep. Gunshots startled him, too, especially during the hot, humid nights when kids roamed like feral cats through the dimly lit streets of Lake Worth. Every night, it seemed, one of them got shot, beaten, stabbed or murdered. No one paid them much attention, though, as long as they didn't try to cross the bridge into Palm Beach. Even legitimate newspapers don't carry stories about crime in Lake Worth unless it involves a misguided tourist getting carjacked. Dwayne imagined dope dealers exchanging gunshots every night on the grass boulevard outside Mar-a-Lago and wondered who the President would sue to keep them quiet.

Dwayne looked at the people around him and was surprised to see among the strangers on the break wall the familiar face and long grey ponytail of Curtis, his foreman from his last job. He was standing near a concrete stairway that led down to a powerboat moored beside a wooden dock. Dwayne thought Curtis had moved with the rest of the road crew to Texas. In the months that had passed since Dwayne's job had ended with the road crew, he'd sold a couple of sculptures at the flea market, and he still had about two hundred American dollars in a paper bag that he stashed in the vegetable drawer of his refrigerator. But even before his brother showed up, he'd begun to wonder if his money would run out before he found another job. He didn't worry about it. Dwayne never worried much about money. He always seemed to have as much as he needed, he told me later, and he felt grateful for what he had. He just wondered where it would come from next.

When Curtis looked in his direction and nodded at him, Dwayne was surprised. "I didn't think Curtis would remember me," he said.

Curtis said he'd left the road crew a few weeks after they'd arrived in Texas. He'd come back to Florida to work for one of his in-laws, who ran a contracting business. The company employed three teams of workers to build and renovate houses in Palm Beach. "We never run out of work," he said.

When Dwayne said he hadn't found a job since he'd left the road crew, Curtis said he should come to work for him. "We can always use a good man," he said. "Even a Canadian." He poked Dwayne in the arm. "Just kidding."

"Cash?" said Dwayne.

Curtis agreed. He said Dwayne could start working on Monday and gave him the address. His crew were renovating a children's playhouse on the property and attaching a solarium to the main house. "Belongs to the Soares family," he said.

That evening Dwayne told his brother that he'd found a job.

"Back to the old grind, eh," said Mike.

"That's one way to look at it," said Dwayne.

"How else would you look at it?" said Mike. "Workin' for the man. Nine to five. All that bullshit."

"You have to start somewhere," said Dwayne. "Curtis is looking for a roofer, too. In case you're interested."

"Roofer," Mike sneered.

"Face it, Mike. You're an ex-con. You're in the country illegally. And this guy offers you a job. I'd say that's pretty lucky."

Mike dismissed Dwayne's comment with a wave of his hand. "You get a job, Slick," he said. "I have other plans."

"They'd better happen soon," said Dwayne. "You can't stay here forever."

Five

In the kitchen the next morning, Dwayne had a slice of bread with butter and a glass of orange juice for breakfast. Then he washed the dishes that Mike had left in the sink the night before. Disturbed by the noise, Mike came into the kitchen wearing only a pair of tight black underpants. When he saw his brother at the sink already dressed in jeans and a short-sleeved shirt, he asked Dwayne where he was going. Dwayne said he was going to church.

Dwayne wasn't especially religious, but he liked to keep his life in order, and attending church helped him to do it. He'd also thought several times about Mary Louise and remembered that her father was the minister at the Church of the Lord Jesus. He decided to go there today. The church was on Johnson Street, she'd said, about ten blocks from his house.

"You think church makes you a better person?" Mike said, sticking a slice of bread into his mouth. Without his dental plate, he chewed awkwardly. "All those hymns and prayers and shit?"

Dwayne shrugged. He didn't want to discuss religion with his brother.

"Never saw the point, myself," said Mike.

"Maybe there is no point," said Dwayne.

"You ask me," Mike said, "you stand around in church to become a better person. You might as well stand around in a garage and become a better car mechanic."

"You might be right," said Dwayne.

"You know anybody at this church?" Mike said.

"The minister's daughter," said Dwayne. "Mary-Louise."

As soon as he said her name, Dwayne wished he'd kept his mouth shut.

"Mary-Louise," said Mike. "Now I get it."

"What's to get?" said Dwayne.

"You're not going to find God," said Mike. "You're going to get laid. So is she your girlfriend or what?"

Dwayne searched for words to describe the reassurance he'd found in church. Lately, he'd felt as if the foundations of his life had come loose beneath his feet and that the structure of his days might crumble, leaving him floundering, exposed and helpless. From one day to the next, he often felt as if he was standing on sand. Pools of warm surf washed over his feet while he ignored the rising tide that could sweep him out to sea. Especially since Mike had arrived, Dwayne had felt the tide rising higher and the sand shifting beneath him. He didn't like the sense of disorder and instability that Mike brought to his life. He didn't like the vague threat to his equilibrium. Mike challenged the way Dwayne lived and forced him to reconsider decisions he'd made about ambition, relationships, money, fate and his place in the world. At church, he might feel himself sheltered for an hour or two from the world's relentless brutality. He could plant his feet firmly and feel himself for at least an hour embraced by a spirit of certainty, love and forgiveness.

"Just a friend," he said.

"Take a lot more than a friend," Mike said, "get me to swallow that God shit."

"It's like you go into someone's kitchen," Dwayne said, knowing that his words would sound ridiculous to his brother, "you smell bread. It didn't just happen by itself."

"Bread," Mike said. "Right." He wandered in his underwear out of the kitchen.

It took Dwayne about half an hour to walk to the church and even then, he wasn't sure that he'd come to the right place. Except for a hand-painted sign by the front door, it looked like any other shabby bungalow in the neighborhood. Clad in faded white clapboard, surrounded by a rusty chain link fence, it stood at the dead end of Johnson Street between a power-line right-of-way and a vacant lot littered with dented appliances and bulging green garbage bags. A small window overlooked a dilapidated car parked on a patch of asphalt.

From inside the building, Dwayne heard voices singing and realized he was late. He stepped inside, thinking he could stand at the back where no one would notice him but, when he opened the door, sunslight flooded into the sanctuary, and about a dozen people turned to look at him. They were standing in the living room of the house in front of three rows of folding chairs that faced the back wall. As he closed the door behind him, Dwayne acknowledged them with a nod of his head and an apologetic grimace. The congregation turned away and continued to sing. He recognized the tune, a hymn called "Gaining Victory Over the World." "We're gathered together before you, as sheep from your pasture we came." Dwayne counted fifteen men and women in the room.

When they stopped singing, Dwayne found an empty chair and sat down. Imitation stained-glass coverings over the windows restricted the daylight from entering the room. Dwayne stared ahead at a framed picture of Jesus on the back wall then looked at the table below the picture where he saw a glass-sided aquarium. A stout man faced the congregation from behind a lectern. He had thinning hair and a pasty-white face as smooth and round as a watermelon. Even in the dim light, Dwayne could see sweat glistening on the man's forehead and cheeks.

When he spoke, the stout man's voice reminded Dwayne of gravel in a tin can. He rattled on about the stain of original sin. The stain covered every human on the planet, he said, from the time he was born until he died. "We are the scum of the earth," he said.

Dwayne listened closely. He'd often felt that he had to apologize for his existence, as if his presence in the midst of other people diminished their lives. He would have removed himself from the world altogether, but he was too curious about the future to kill himself and he couldn't endure more than a day or two of solitude before he went looking for someone to remind him that he was part of a bigger world. That's why he liked going to the coffee shop, why he sat with the fishermen on the wall along Flagler Drive, and went to the flea market on Sunday. It was another reason why he'd come to church this morning. He felt apologetic even now for intruding on the lives of other people. He had no confidence that they would welcome his intrusion, and he tried to make himself as small as possible as he insinuated himself into a corner of the room.

As the service continued, the men and women in the congregation heaved themselves to their feet to sing and pray and then folded themselves onto their hard-backed chairs again, grimacing as they stood up and sat down as if they had bad hips, sore backs and arthritic knees. Dwayne figured they were in pain. That was often why people went to church. He knew from experience that pain could remove the good humor from a person's life. He'd once thrown his back out while carrying a friend's refrigerator out of his apartment. For about two weeks, he could hardly move. That had made him grumpy, although he'd directed most of his ill-temper toward himself for being so stupid as to carry a refrigerator down a flight of stairs. Pride, that's what it was. Dwayne had been too proud to admit that he couldn't do the job himself, and look where it got him: two weeks lying flat on his back, popping pain killers and peeing into a milk jug. Dwayne wasn't sure if the people in the congregation were injured, sick or grieving, but he figured they felt angry for a good reason, even if he didn't know what it was, and he vowed not to do or say anything to offend them and make them feel even worse.

Dwayne studied the backs of the five women in the congregation, but didn't recognize Mary Louise until he looked more closely at the woman seated at the piano. She was wearing a shapeless grey dress that seemed several sizes too big for her, and her hair covered her neck, but hers was the only body that didn't bulge like a hernia over the back of her chair. When she spotted him in the back row, she turned her head to smile at him quickly. He wondered why she'd changed her appearance so drastically until he remembered what she'd said at the flea market about getting a tattoo "where daddy couldn't see it."

Her daddy began reading aloud an essay about friendship: "For what person is there, in the name of gods and men, who would wish to be surrounded by unlimited wealth and to abound in every material blessing, on condition that he love no one and that no one love him? Such indeed is the life of tyrants in which there can be no faith, no affection, no trust in the continuance of goodwill; where every act arouses suspicion and anxiety and where friendship has no place."

Friendship, he said, depended not on a person's wealth or appearance. "Take my daughter," he said, looking toward Mary Louise. "She'll never win no beauty contest. But she don't mind, do you, sweetie? That's cuz she has friends. And what could be more beautiful than friendship?"

When the sermon ended, a skinny man in an over-sized suit passed a collection plate through the congregation. When it came to Dwayne, he opened his wallet and put a five-dollar bill on the plate. The skinny man carried the plate to the table in front of the preacher.

Looking down at the meager collection of bills and coins, the preacher reached into the glass-sided aquarium on the table. With both hands, he pulled out a lizard and raised it above his head. The lizard was as big as a loaf of bread. Even in the dim light, Dwayne could see its legs moving and its tongue like a live wire flicking in and out, but the creature didn't struggle. Holding the lizard aloft, the preacher closed his eyes and led the congregation in a short prayer. After he returned the lizard to the aquarium, he recited a valediction.

At the end of the service, the congregation moped and shuffled their way to the front door, where the preacher waited to shake their hands and offer his blessing. Even in daylight, he seemed undefined and colorless, like an unfinished drawing, one of those people who, even on the brightest day of summer, never seems fully illuminated.

When Dwayne introduced himself, the minister welcomed him to the church and said his name was Pastor Bob. "Last name's Hobsbawn," he said, "but nobody uses it."

Dwayne said he'd enjoyed the sermon. He'd especially liked the passages about friendship, he said.

"Cicero," said Pastor Bob. "Marcus Tullius Cicero."

He said he'd never seen Dwayne before and asked where he'd come from. "Canada," Dwayne said.

Pastor Bob cocked his enormous head.

"Can't think of nothing off the top of my head we should know about Canada."

"Justin Bieber?" said Dwayne.

"What's that?" said Pastor Bob.

"Or Robertson screwdrivers," Dwayne said.

Pastor Bob looked perplexed. "Don't know either one of those things."

"They have a square tip, fit into a square hole on the screw top," Dwayne said. "Maybe you can't get them here."

"You mean a square-head," said Pastor Bob.

"Maybe," said Dwayne.

"We got those, all right. You get 'em at Home Depot."

"Pretty sure they're Canadian," said Dwayne.

"Didn't know they were called Biebers," said Pastor Bob.

"Bieber's the singer," said Dwayne. "The screwdriver's a Robertson."

"You know about tools?" said Pastor Bob, lighting a cigarette.

"A bit," said Dwayne, startled to see a minister smoking at the door to his own church. He was glad when Mary Louise came to the doorway and stood beside him, although her plain grey dress disturbed him. It looked sinister, like a shroud on the Venus de Milo, imputing evil where he'd seen only beauty and innocence. A pair of glasses hung from a chain around her neck. A big black purse hung from a strap over her shoulder. On her feet, she wore black lace-up shoes with round toes. She'd removed her earrings and the gold stud from her nose. But Dwayne still saw the promise in her blue eyes.

"Dwayne made the lizard," she said.

"Is that so?" said Pastor Bob. "You some kind of artist?"

"Sort of," Dwayne shrugged.

"You know Rollo Barnes?"

"No sir," said Dwayne. "Your daughter mentioned him."

"Local artist," said Pastor Bob. "You make much money from your lizards, Dwayne?"

"Not much," said Dwayne.

"Barnes makes good money," said Pastor Bob. "'Course, it helps, he's rich to begin with." He looked at Mary Louise. "You should introduce Dwayne to your friend. The gallery guy."

"Darius Pierre," said Mary Louise.

"That lizard has a life of its own," said Pastor Bob. "How'd you do that?"

"Just happens," said Dwayne.

"He's being modest," said Mary Louise.

Pastor Bob ignored his daughter. "Not much sense in doing it, you can't make money. You sell many?"

"A few," said Dwayne. And then, hoping to leave a good impression on Mary Louise, he said, "The Soares family might buy one."

"Sure," said Pastor Bob. "If pigs could fly, right, son?"

Dwayne felt his face turning hot with embarrassment and regretted the lie.

"You should meet that guy Darius," said Pastor Bob. Smoke drifted from his mouth, as if he'd swallowed a small bonfire. "If anybody can make money from art, that guy can. Ain't that right, honey?"

"Bet he'd sell your lizards," said Mary Louise. "For more than ten dollars, too."

A small man limped up to Pastor Bob and coughed to get his attention. Pastor Bob tossed his cigarette butt onto the asphalt and squashed it under his shoe, as if to signal that he'd lost all interest in Dwayne, his lizards and his lies.

Dwayne started to walk away, but Mary Louise caught up to him. "Where you going?" she said.

"Home," said Dwayne.

"You driving?"

Dwayne said he'd walked to the church.

"I'll go with you," she said. "We can take the bus."

They walked together to a glass-walled bus shelter by the Dixie Highway. Inside, Mary Louise took a scrunchy from her purse and folded her hair into a pile on top of her head. She kicked off her shoes and turned her back to Dwayne.

"Unzip me," she said.

She let the dress fall around her ankles. Underneath, she was wearing a short black T-shirt that left her midriff bare and a black leather skirt.

Her toenails were painted purple. From her purse she took a pair of jeweled sandals, which she pulled onto her feet. She pulled rings onto each of her fingers.

"Christ," she said. "What a pain in the ass."

She was stuffing the dress and shoes into her bag as the bus pulled up to the curb. Dwayne paid for both of them with the remaining cash in his wallet. "It's only two bucks," he said, when Mary Louise protested.

"You could make a lot more than that from Darius," she said when she slid onto a seat near the front of the bus. She pulled eyeliner and a compact mirror from her purse.

"I don't really care about the money," said Dwayne, sitting down beside her.

"That's stupid," said Mary Louise. "Everybody wants money."

"I'm not stupid," he said.

"Then why don't you want money?"

From the tone of her voice, Dwayne felt as if he'd offended her.

"I know people need it," he said. "But I don't live for it."

"If I had more money, I'd never work again," said Mary Louise.

"Where do you work?" said Dwayne.

"Starbucks," she said. "At the Gardens Mall. Just on weekends. Daddy doesn't like me working on school nights."

When they got off the bus at 10th Avenue, Dwayne guided Mary Louise through the neighborhood of small houses and converted trailers to North K Street. The sun was hot, the ground was dry, and there were no shade trees.

"Will you come to church again?" she said.

"Probably," Dwayne said.

"I can't stop," said Mary Louise. "Daddy always guides me back to the Lord Jesus Christ, and Our Savior always forgives me."

Dwayne nodded. "Forgiveness," he said.

"Not like those cocksuckers in Palm Beach," said Mary Louise. Her words startled Dwayne. "See, there I go again."

"Again what?" said Dwayne.

"Falling."

"Falling?"

"Weren't you listening, silly? Falling from grace. And it's all your fault."

"I'm not doing anything."

"I can hear the Brothers Four," Mary-Louise said.

"You have brothers?" said Dwayne.

"They're singers."

"Your brothers?"

"The Brothers Four. I always hear the Brothers Four when I'm with a man like you, just before I fall. They're singing 'Green Fields'."

"I don't hear anything," Dwayne said.

Mary Louise started to sing. "Once there were green fields kissed by the sun." She said, "It's a sad song."

Dwayne said he'd never heard it before.

"I only know there's nothing here for me," Mary-Louise warbled as she leaned against him. "Oh, catch me, Dwayne. I'm falling."

And she did. She would have fallen onto the sidewalk if Dwayne hadn't caught her. She felt warm and compliant in his arms. She pressed her body against him. Dwayne could feel her breasts through her T-shirt.

Dwayne sensed her need for his physical affirmation, and it disturbed him. With his hands against her waist, he extended his arms and looked at her.

"How old are you?" he said.

"Eighteen," she said.

"You don't look eighteen."

"In January."

"January three years from now, maybe," he said.

She smiled. "People say I'm mature for my age."

"Doesn't mean you're mature just because you look older."

"I know what I'm doing," she said.

"You shouldn't be doing this," said Dwayne.

"Doing what?"

"You know. This. Having sex with older men."

"We're not having sex."

"That's what you want, isn't it?"

"You're not that old," she said.

"I'm a lot older than you."

"Who says I want to have sex with you?"

"Don't you?"

"Maybe."

"So wait till you're older."

"Don't you like me?"

"Of course I like you. That's why you should wait till you're older."

"How old should I be?"

"Older than you are now."

"What am I supposed to do till then?"

"I don't know. Stuff that girls do. Dancing. Playing with your dog. Riding your bike. Studying nuclear physics. Writing letters for Amnesty International. Making snow angels."

"There's no snow here."

"Sand angels, then. Learning to play basketball. Reading a book. How do I know? I'm not a girl. Lying under a tree, looking at the sky. Making fun of old people who try to look like young people."

"Sounds boring."

"Better than what you're doing now."

"Why?"

"Because you grow up too fast, and then you wish you'd spent more time being a kid."

"I hate being a kid."

"You'll be old soon."

"And I'll have money to do whatever I want."

"From working at Starbucks?"

"From having sex with older men," she said.

"I'm not going to pay you," said Dwayne.

"You won't," she said, "but men do. They're a lot older than you. A lot richer, too."

Dwayne shook his head.

"Just kidding," said Mary Louise. "I'm going to be a model."

Dwayne had grown up with players on his hockey team who thought they were good enough to become professionals. They'd been so sure of themselves, so cocky in their estimation of their talents. None of them had made it. Now they worked in shoe stores, drove trucks or spent eight hours a day in meetings and pushing papers around on a desk. It seemed that ambition led only to disappointment and regret. But was failure a reason not to dream?

"It's good to have a dream," he said without conviction.

"Mister Kleppman says I look like Gigi Hadid."

"Who's she?" said Dwayne.

"A famous model. She makes a million dollars a month."

"And Mister Kleppman?"

"A rich man," she said. "He gave me these earrings. He knows an agent in New York. He said he'd take me there. You wait. When I'm rich, I'll buy another one of your lizards. Then you'll be rich, and famous, too."

They turned onto North K Street and walked toward Dwayne's house. His brother was sitting on the front steps and watched them as they approached.

"We still have to talk to Darius," Mary Louise said.

"Right," said Dwayne.

"How about tomorrow?" said Mary Louise.

"I have to work."

They stood together in front of Mike on the steps.

"Tuesday, then," said Mary Louise. "I'll tell Darius to meet us. Pick me up before you go."

"Darius?" said Mike.

"At the gallery," Mary Louise said.

Mike nodded. "Darius Pierre," he said.

"You know him?" said Mary Louise.

"Runs the M2 Gallery," said Mike.

He sounded as if he knew all about the gallery, the man and where precisely they fit into the matrix of the art world.

"This is my brother," Dwayne interjected.

Mike nodded at Mary Louise, running his eyes over her breasts, the jewel in her navel, her hips and her legs down to her painted toenails, then looking at her face. Dwayne could tell from his posture that his brother had liked what he'd seen.

"I'm Mike," he said. "You must be Mary Louise."

"Mike just got here," said Dwayne.

"How do you two know each other?" Mike said.

"We're friends," said Dwayne.

"He sold me one of his sculptures," said Mary Louise.

"One of these?"

Dwayne hadn't noticed the lizard beside Mike until his brother held it up. Mary Louise nodded.

"How much did he charge for it?" Mike said.

"Ten dollars," said Mary Louise.

"I should have given it to you," said Dwayne.

"I would have paid more," said Mary Louise.

"Like I say," Dwayne said, "I don't do it for the money."

"How's that workin' out?" said Mike.

"I get more than money at the flea market," said Dwayne.

"What else?" Mike said.

"If it wasn't for the flea market, I wouldn't have met Mary Louise."

"Dwayne doesn't know shit about money," said Mike.

"And you do?" said Dwayne.

"I know enough to want more of it," said Mike. "Unlike you."

He looked again at Mary Louise. "Anybody ever tell you, you look like Gigi Hadid?" He looked at Dwayne. "She's a model," he said, as if he was translating a foreign language.

"I know," said Dwayne.

"You think so?" said Mary Louise.

"She's hot," said Mike.

"Everyone says that," said Mary Louise.

"They're right," said Mike. "Turn around."

Mary Louise did as he told her.

"You've got the same figure," he said.

"I'm taking a modeling course," said Mary Louise.

"At school?" said Dwayne.

"Online," said Mary Louise. "It cost two hundred dollars. Mister Kleppman gave me the money. What time is it?"

Mary Louise said she had to go to work.

"I'll drive you," said Mike. He stood up then and escorted Mary Louise to the Datsun in the driveway.

"Want the keys?" said Dwayne.

Mike held up the keys. "Got 'em," he said.

Dwayne watched Mary Louise shut the door and slide closer to Mike as he backed the truck out of the driveway. When he turned to go into the house, he picked up the sculpture where Mike had left it on the steps.

Six

When Dwayne went to bed, his brother hadn't returned from taking Mary Louise to work, and he was still gone the next morning. Without his truck, Dwayne rode his bicycle across the bridge to the Soares house on El Brillo Way.

Before they started, Curtis reminded his crew that they were under strict orders to stay on the work site, not talk to the staff and never look directly at a member of the Soares family. Anyone who violated the rules, he said, would be instantly dismissed. That didn't bother Dwayne. He preferred not to talk to people at all.

One of his co-workers told him that the Soares family were "big in root beer, in South America." Dwayne imagined a fleet of shiny trucks loaded with wooden cases of pop bottles, driven along a four-lane highway by happy members of the Soares family, each wearing a windbreaker with the company logo on the chest. It would have surprised him if you'd told him how much work it took to build an empire based on soft drinks in South America: the competitors who needed to be acquired or defeated; the outstretched palms that needed to be greased; the connections that needed to be cultivated; the family hierarchies that had to be respected; the extortionate demands that had to be met from criminals, social activists and priests; the interminable negotiations with banks, government officials, suppliers, multinational conglomerates, insurance companies and municipal utilities; the petty quibbling of compliant union leaders that had to be addressed to keep thirty thousand employees coming to work every day. That, in a nutshell, was the difference between Dwayne and the people in Palm Beach like the Soares family, who would unwittingly become collectors of his work. He didn't understand their world any better than they understood his.

Dwayne had just started working that morning, unloading bundles of specialty floor tiles from the back of a truck for installation in the playhouse, when Curtis told him to stop. He said Dwayne would need a voluntary identification card. "People here don't like strangers hanging around their property," Curtis said. "You probably won't need it, though, being Canadian."

"I know what it is," Dwayne said, remembering the cop who'd stopped him when he'd driven his brother early one morning through Palm Beach.

Curtis drove him to the police headquarters on South County Road. The card cost fifteen dollars and confirmed that Dwayne had a job and a reason for being in the town.

Dwayne glanced at the photo on the card. Like most of us when we look at a photograph of ourselves, he thought his face looked goofy: flat and pock-marked, with puffy cheeks, big chin, ears the size of ashtrays. One of the weird people on the planet. No wonder women showed no interest in him, he thought. Well, that was their loss, he told himself, but he didn't really believe it. He thought of Mary Louise. He looked forward to seeing her again.

When he rode home that night on his bicycle, the truck was in the driveway.

"Where the fuck did you go?" Dwayne said when he found his brother in the kitchen.

"Business," said Mike. He was opening and closing the cupboards.

"What kind of business?"

"Gonna make us all rich." Mike moved to the refrigerator and opened the door.

"I had to go to work on my bicycle," Dwayne said

"Don't worry," said Mike, pulling open the vegetable crisper. "The way this works, you'll have money to buy ten bicycles. And another fucking truck. Yours is a piece of shit."

He picked up the paper bag where Dwayne stored his cash. "You got any food in this place?"

Mike said he hadn't eaten in two days.

"We better go get some dinner," Dwayne said.

Mike put the bag back in the drawer and closed the fridge. They went outside and got into Dwayne's truck and drove a few blocks to the Dunkin Donuts on 10th Avenue, where they sat at the counter and ordered club sandwiches and coffee.

"You gotta find a job, Mike," said Dwayne while they waited for their food.

"I gotta make some money," said Mike.

"How else can you make money," said Dwayne, "except you get a job and work for it?"

"There are better ways," said Mike.

"I've never found a better way."

"That's because you don't know how to do it," said Mike.

"That's because I don't give a shit," said Dwayne.

"Everybody gives a shit about money," said Mike.

"Long as I have enough, I'm happy," said Dwayne.

"You don't have the gift," Mike said.

"What gift?" said Dwayne.

"For making money."

"And you do?"

"Correct," said Mike.

The waitress brought their food on plates that she placed on the counter in front of them.

"You've always got a scheme to make us all rich," Dwayne said, "but you always use other people's money to do it." He asked his brother how he intended to make money this time.

Mike said he had lots of good ideas. All he needed was an investor with a few thousand dollars to grease the wheels. After that, he said, it was just a matter of time.

"That's why I'm here," he said.

"Here?"

"In Palm Beach," said Mike. "It's where the money is."

"You're not there yet."

"I will be, dude. You wait. I have the gift."

Dwayne rolled his eyes. How many times had he listened to Mike's bullshit? That and the violence were two of the reasons he didn't like to spend time with his brother.

"It's like being left-handed," Mike said. "You either have it or you don't."

"Some gift," said Dwayne. "You just spent the last two years in prison."

"The pursuit of happiness, baby," said Mike. "You gotta take a risk."

Dwayne knew all about the risks that Mike took: selling drugs, fencing stolen property, importing counterfeit designer jeans. "That's not risk," said Dwayne. "That's crime."

"That's the thing, Dwayne. We're different. You want money, but you won't put your life on the line to get it."

Dwayne said again that Mike needed to get a job. "You can't live with me forever."

His brother laughed. "We've been through this before," he said. Jobs were for suckers, he said. He intended to get rich, he said, and a man didn't get rich by working nine to five. "And don't worry," he said. "I'll be gone before the end of the week."

"Promise?" said Dwayne.

"Guaranteed," said Mike.

The waitress held a coffee pot over Mike's cup and asked if he wanted more. Mike ignored her. She asked Dwayne. He said, "No, thanks." She tore two pages from her pad and left a bill on the counter in front of each of them. Mike slid his toward Dwayne.

"I'll pay you back," he said.

Dwayne left fifteen dollars on the counter. When the waitress brought change, he left it beside his plate for a tip. When he turned away from the counter, Mike scooped up the change and put it in his pocket.

Back at the house, Mike removed the plate from his mouth where his front teeth used to be. He'd lost them after a truck cut him off in traffic and he challenged the driver to a fight. The driver had hit Mike in the mouth with a crowbar. He placed the teeth on the windowsill among Dwayne's carvings and picked up the figure of a lizard.

"So here's my plan," he said.

Dwayne rolled his eyes. "What's your plan this time, Mike?"

"I'm gonna take your fucking lizards to that guy Darius, runs the art gallery."

"In Palm Beach," said Dwayne.

"Correct. And I'm gonna make him pay me what they're worth."

"How much do you think they're worth?"

"More than ten bucks. I know that much."

Dwayne shook his head. He was about to tell Mike not to touch his sculptures, but he changed his mind. He'd made the pieces with his own hands. They weren't fake. They weren't counterfeit. They weren't stolen. Dwayne didn't think his brother would get much money for them, but at least he wouldn't get arrested for trying.

"Okay," said Dwayne.

"I'll need the truck," said Mike. "Just for tomorrow."

"The one you said was a piece of shit."

"It'll do," said Mike. "I'll drop you at work. And then I'll pick up Mary Louise."

"She's going with you?" said Dwayne.

"It was her idea," said Mike.

When Dwayne went to bed that night, he resisted contemplating the possibility that his brother could sell his work. But as his thoughts drifted into realms of speculation, fantasy and dreams, he imagined the impression that he would make on Mary Louise when she saw that he had money.

Seven

Dwayne spent the next day at work resisting the hope he felt that the M2 Gallery might represent his work. If he received the endorsement of a legitimate dealer, perhaps he could call himself an artist without wondering if he really was. But hope inevitably led to disappointment, and he'd felt disappointed enough in his life to know that doubt was the better option.

By the time he rode home, he doubted that any of his hopes would come true. He certainly knew better than to place any hope in his brother. But the sight of the Datsun in the driveway rekindled his anticipation. Dwayne dropped his bike on the lawn, took three strides to the front door, then walked nonchalantly into the kitchen, where he found Mike at the table with Mary Louise. There was a bottle of wine and two half-filled juice glasses on the table.

"You're home," he said.

"Hi, Dwayne," said Mary Louise. She was wearing a sweater and leggings. The temperature had fallen again.

"Good day?" said Dwayne.

"Dope," said Mary Louise, raising her glass and laughing as she looked across the table at Mike. Her laughter sounded forced. Dwayne wondered if she was drunk.

Mike picked up an envelope from the table and held it out to Dwayne.

"What's this?" Dwayne said.

"Money," Mike said.

Dwayne looked inside the envelope at five twenty-dollar bills.

"He bought one of your lizards," Mike said.

"There's a hundred dollars here," said Dwayne.

"You'll get more when he sells it," said Mike.

"Darius says you should quit your job," said Mary Louise.

Dwayne noticed for the first time that she was holding a little white dog in her lap.

"Why would I do that?" he said. "I just started."

"Doesn't matter," said Mike.

"'Course it matters," said Dwayne. "Curtis needs me. And I need the money."

Curtis had even paid him that day in cash. Dwayne didn't want to let him down.

"I thought you didn't need money," said Mike.

"Everybody needs it."

"Whatever," Mary Louise said. "But you should quit."

"You got a better idea?" said Dwayne.

"Yeah," said Mary Louise.

She handed Dwayne a magazine. "Look at this," she said.

Dwayne leaned back against the counter and leafed through the pages. He didn't read the text, but he looked at the photographs. "What's this stuff?' he said.

"Art, silly," said Mary Louise. She giggled.

Dwayne closed the magazine.

"Look at page thirty-seven," said Mary Louise.

Dwayne turned to page thirty-seven. "This supposed to mean something?"

"Your stuff's just as good," she said.

"Maybe," said Dwayne. "So what?"

"You know how much they pay for that shit?" said Mary Louise.

Dwayne looked at the page. "Don't know," he said. "There's no price."

"You want the price, you have to go to the gallery," said Mike.

"Says here the gallery's in Tucson," said Dwayne.

"There's galleries right here in Palm Beach, sell the same shit," Mike said.

"No shit," said Dwayne.

"Seriously," said Mary Louise. "How much do you get for one of those lizards?"

"Ten bucks."

Mary Louise tapped her finger on the catalogue. "In a gallery like that, lots of fancy customers. You could charge ten, twenty, a hundred times more."

"Says who?"

"Says Darius."

"The gallery guy," Dwayne said.

"You know who he lives with?" said Mike.

"Who?"

"Melanie Merriwether."

"Who's Melanie Merriwether?"

"Just the richest woman in, like, the world," said Mary Louise.

"So this guy Darius," said Dwayne.

"He likes your alligators," said Mike. "He wants you to make more."

"Lizards," said Dwayne.

"He says he can sell one to Keith Kleppman."

"Who?"

"Some rich dude," said Mike.

"I told you about him," said Mary Louise.

"That's why you have to quit your job," said Mike.

Dwayne felt flattered that Mary Louise thought he might have enough talent to support himself by selling his art.

"What if he can't sell them?"

"He can sell them," Mary Louise said. "He sells all sorts of weird shit."

"I just got my job," said Dwayne. "I can't quit now."

Mary Louise held up a tube of colored stone chips. "He says you should use these," she said.

"What are these?" Dwayne said.

"Emeralds. Rubies," said Mike.

"He says Mister Kleppman likes jewels," said Mary Louise.

Dwayne stood beside Mary Louise and looked at the colored chips in the tube.

"You put them down one side," she said. She reached out and stroked Dwayne's ribs through his T-shirt. Dwayne, who was ticklish, flinched. "Like skin," she said.

"Pavé," said Dwayne.

"Right," said Mary Louise. With an exaggerated accent, she said, "Pavé."

Dwayne looked again at the colored stones.

"How am I supposed to do it?" Dwayne said.

"The fuck should we know?" said Mike. "Crazy glue, maybe? And make a bigger one. Maybe use that log on the front lawn. Darius says people like 'em big."

Dwayne returned to the counter. "I won't do it," he said.

"What do you mean, you won't do it?"

"I can't."

He started to explain how he felt, that gemstones had no place in his work, that he had to follow his heart. But the words didn't sound convincing, and he could tell from the expression on Mary Louise's face that he was making no sense. His brother shook his head and scowled.

"That's bullshit," said Mike.

"It's true," said Dwayne.

"Fuck you," said Mike.

"Suit yourself," said Dwayne.

"Why do you have to be so fucking virtuous?" Mike said.

"Got a better idea?" said Dwayne.

"Some of us just want to get laid," said Mike. He looked at Mary Louise. She looked down at the dog in her lap.

"You always this serious?" she said.

"Me?" said Dwayne.

"Yeah," she said.

"It's not about me," said Dwayne. "My art."

"Your art," scoffed Mike. "Fucking alligators."

"Lizards," Dwayne said.

"Doesn't sound like you have much fun," said Mary Louise.

"What's fun got to do with it?"

"If it pays, it's fun," said Mike. "Does it pay?"

"Not really," said Dwayne.

"Right," said Mike. "So why not put the fucking jewels on the fucking alligator – lizard, whatever – make some money?"

"Why should I do that?" Dwayne said.

Mary Louise said, "You could spend it on me."

"And this guy Darius, he'll pay me how much?"

"Three, four hundred," Mike said.

"Each?"

"Each."

"Why can't he sell them without jewels?"

"He says people like jewels," said Mary Louise.

"I don't like jewels," said Dwayne.

"You gotta give the customer what he wants," said Mike.

"Think what you could buy," said Mary Louise.

"Like what?" said Dwayne.

Mary Louise looked at her dog. The psoriatic mutt reminded Dwayne of a worn-out wash mitt. The dog nibbled with teeth the size of rice grains on her hand.

"Jeff," Mike said. "No biting."

From the way he spoke to the dog, Dwayne realized that his brother had spent more time that he'd thought with Mary Louise. Until now, Dwayne hadn't known that she even had a dog.

"That bracelet I saw?" said Mary Louise, looking at Mike.

"What bracelet?" said Dwayne.

"In that jewellery store on Worth Avenue. Kauffmann de Suisse?"

"You could buy yourself a new truck," said Mike.

"You could take me to New York," said Mary Louise.

"Needs work," said Mike.

"Why would I go there?" Dwayne said.

"We could buy a penthouse. See the whole city from our bedroom. I could be a model. Mister Kleppman says he'll take me someday."

Her fantasies made Dwayne feel sad. "I like it here," he said.

"We could live here, too," she said, "if we had the money."

"How much does it take?"

"Guy named Nelson Pelz?" said Mike. "His property taxes are two million dollars."

"No kidding," said Dwayne.

"That's why I want to be rich," said Mary Louise.

"So you can pay taxes?"

"So I can do whatever I want."

Mike looked at Mary Louise. "See," he said, tilting his head toward Dwayne while looking at her face. "I told you. He's a fucking idiot."

Dwayne thought about selling his sculptures for a lot of money, but even as he thought about it, his stomach felt uncomfortable. Money confused him. It made him think that he mattered more than he'd mattered without it. That seemed to be a dangerous way to think. His stepfather in Petrolia was obsessed with money and possessions, as if they distinguished him from other men and endowed him with superior attributes. He bought watches, kitchen appliances, bedroom suites, power tools, bicycles, patio furniture and sports equipment for rock-bottom prices from people who didn't know or didn't care about the value of the stuff they were selling. He bought used cars and pissed off his neighbors on weekends when he revved the cars' engines under their bedroom windows on Oozlovsky Street when they were trying to sleep. He didn't care. Why should he? He had more possessions than they did. He was in a different class. He measured other people by the brand of their ski jacket or the price of their snowmobile. He encouraged Dwayne to make friends with boys in his class who lived in the biggest houses and whose fathers drove the fanciest cars. Once he realized that Dwayne had no interest in money, his stepfather treated him as if he were mentally deficient.

Watching his mother squander her affection on that asshole had driven

Dwayne to distraction. His emotions had run wild, like squirrels darting through trees. Dwayne might have lived under the same roof as Howard Rondell, but he refused to share his values. He could make fun of Dwayne, criticize him, laugh at him or ignore him, but he would never persuade him to regard money as anything but a curse and a symptom of evil. Only his carving had kept his thoughts focused.

"The trouble is," he said now, "I think there are lots of other things in life besides money."

"Not for me," said Mary Louise, looking across the table at Mike. "I want to be rich."

And as she said the words, Dwayne watched her transform before his eyes from a woman of limitless promise into someone ordinary and pedestrian. It happened in an instant, the way the lights go out when the power fails. He wondered against all his conscious intentions if this woman's affection was worth the compromises that she wanted him to make.

"You remind me of my brother," he said.

"Nothing wrong with that, baby," said Mike.

"He thinks there is," said Mary Louise.

"I just wonder why you'd settle for such a paltry ambition," said Dwayne, "when there's so much more to aim for."

"You sound like my father," said Mary Louise.

"Get your head out of your ass, Dwayne," said Mike.

Dwayne looked again at the chips of ruby and emerald in his hand. "How many?"

"As many as you can do in a couple of weeks."

"I don't know," he said.

Mary Louise said she had to go. She was working that afternoon in Lantana. "And then I have to get ready for the party," she said.

"What party?" said Dwayne.

"I just said. Kleppman's." She shrugged. "He has these parties. I bring my friends."

"Like a recruiter," said Dwayne.

"Something like that."

"Like a pimp's more like it," said Mike. He stood up. "I'll drive you."

He looked at Dwayne. "Don't forget. One bigger lizard. Kleppman likes them big. Darius says."

Dwayne watched the Datsun back out of the driveway. The engine rattled with a sound that reminded him of a chest cold. He flinched when his brother floored the accelerator. From the passenger seat, Mary Louise waved at him. The truck lurched forward toward Lake Avenue.

Dwayne looked again at the colored stones. He felt as if he was wasting his time. The anticipation that he'd felt a moment ago turned into the more familiar feeling of resignation. He felt humiliated, as if he'd duped himself into thinking that he might have a chance to become an artist instead of a lackey. He knew his place in the world. He was a practical man. A practical man compromised himself to get along. He qualified his dreams with common sense and tempered his hope with the more certain expectation of failure. He decided to find a way to attach the gemstones to his carvings, even if it felt like putting wheels on a fish.

He went outside and retrieved the mahogany log. He'd never worked with mahogany. He wondered what he'd find as he peeled away the layers. It would probably take him days or weeks, but he'd give his brother what he wanted. He wouldn't expect much in return. He had enough to deal with in his life without anticipating more disappointment.

Back in the house, he went to the refrigerator and found the paper bag where he stored his cash. Into the bag he stuffed the bills that he'd received that day, a few hundred from Curtis and another hundred from his brother. He didn't count the cash in the bag, but he felt reassured to see that the bag was getting full.

He went to the front door again and looked out at the lawn. Preoccupied with the arguments in his mind about the sculptures, the jewels and his brother's relationship with Mary Louise, he hadn't noticed until now that someone had stolen his bicycle.

Eight

In his weeks on the job, Dwayne learned first-hand about the excesses of the Soares family. He spent his first three days helping a cabinet maker install cedar paneling in a second-floor room off the master bedroom. The cedar-paneled room covered an area almost as big as Dwayne's house in Lake Worth, although it had no windows and only one door. Dwayne assumed it was a den or a child's playroom, and he was surprised when the carpenter told him it would become Mrs. Soares's shoe closet. It seemed incomprehensible to Dwayne that you would need an entire room to store your shoes. In Petrolia, a schoolmate had shown Dwayne his father's collection of fishing lures, which the man kept in a cabinet in his garage: poppers, jigs, spinners, spoons, plugs, flies; flashes of silver and gold, streaks of bright red, blue and green, feathers and thread and sharp barbed hooks. Far more lures than a person could ever use in a lifetime. Dwayne's schoolmate said that his father seldom went fishing. He just liked to collect lures. Dwayne figured that Mrs. Soares had fallen victim to a similar obsession. Long after he finished working on the house, he thought of that room and imagined it filled with shoes as varied and colorful as fishing lures.

Most of Dwayne's co-workers were dark-haired, brown-skinned Mexicans. They knew that Dwayne came from Canada, and they figured that, with his blonde hair and blue eyes, he was remote and cold because he'd grown up so close to the Arctic Circle, like a Viking. He seemed unassuming and mild-mannered. He worked hard and seemed friendly enough, in a silent way, but he didn't engage in small talk, didn't banter with his mates about women, football or cars, and didn't show much interest in their chitchat, most of which they conducted in Spanish. At noon, he perched himself on a stack of cinder blocks in the shade of the playhouse, where he ate his lunch, stared at the palm trees, removed a piece of wood from a plastic shopping bag and applied one of his sharp-edged tools to it like a surgeon performing an operation. His co-workers wondered about the surly dead-eyed hoodlum who sometimes drove him to work in the morning. He didn't look at all like Dwayne. They would have been surprised to know that the man was Dwayne's brother.

Over the weeks that Dwayne spent carving the big lizard, his brother spent less time at the house on North K Street. Sometimes he didn't come home for days. When Dwayne asked him one morning where he'd gone, Mike said he'd been spending time with a new friend. "Guy named Shirko." Occasionally, he borrowed the truck. On those days, since Dwayne no longer had a bicycle, Mike drove him to work.

On one of these mornings, a Thursday in December, they were sitting in the Datsun with the windows rolled down, waiting for a long line of cars on Southern Boulevard to cross the bridge over the inland waterway into Palm Beach. Between seven-thirty and nine on weekday mornings, there are so many workmen, sales clerks, Cuban cleaning ladies, Mexican gardeners and Ivy League pool boys heading across the single-lane bridge that they create a traffic jam. In the evening they conduct a similar migration back to the modest homes that they maintain with their labors.

Most of them like to work in Palm Beach. They get paid well to spend their days in a pleasant environment and, if it bothers them that it takes them a year to earn what their employers and clients earn in a few hours, they have the satisfaction of looking down their noses and raising their eyebrows at the pointless extravagance of the rich.

This morning, Mike surprised Dwayne when he said, "I'll be moving out soon."

"You get a job?" said Dwayne.

"No," said Mike. "I found a place to live. Heard about it from Mary Louise."

"You bought it?"

"Renting."

"You need money?" said Dwayne.

"Got some," said Mike.

"How'd that happen?"

"We put a few deals together."

"We?"

"Me and Shirko."

"Your new pal."

Dwayne thought of asking for details about the deals. He wondered if they involved selling dope or persuading someone in a bar to front the money to buy a freighter load of coffee beans, maybe buy the freighter itself. But he realized that he didn't really want to know.

"Where's your place?" he said.

"Lantana," said Mike. "Hypoluxo Road. It's a one bedroom."

"Cool," said Dwayne. He let out a breath of relief. His shoulders relaxed. He hadn't realized until this moment that he'd felt so anxious about his brother's continual presence in his life.

"Gonna get a car, too," said Mike. "Got a line on a Challenger. Pretty sure I can get it for a song."

"That's great."

"So you can keep this shitbox."

Dwayne didn't acknowledge the insult or quibble over his brother's in-gratitude. He just felt relieved that his brother would soon move out of the house.

A few days later, Dwayne finished the mahogany carving and applied the colored stones along its flanks, just as Mike had ordered. He applied them, as well, to two others that he'd brought with him from Canada. He thought they looked ridiculous, like pants on a dog, but Mike said they looked "sensational."

"What now?" said Dwayne. He remembered the day clearly. He'd just come home from work with more cash in his pocket from Curtis.

"I'll call Darius," said Mike.

When he reached the gallery, he told Darius to come to the house. He waited at the front door with the sculptures in a bag. When Darius pulled up in the mauve Aston Martin, Mike stepped outside. Darius took the sculptures and walked back to the car.

"Hold on," Mike said. "I'll go with you."

Dwayne watched from the window as Mike folded himself into the front seat. He remembered watching his brother's profile as the car passed the house. He remembered watching the fancy car until it disappeared around the corner at the end of the street. He didn't think at the time that he would never see his brother again. He went into the kitchen. He took the cash out of his pocket and opened the refrigerator. He took the paper bag out of the vegetable crisper, but when he looked inside, it was empty.

PART THREE

"He who knows a thousand works of art knows a thousand frauds."
Horace

One

The police tried to figure out how Celeste ended up dead on South Ocean Boulevard outside Keith Kleppman's home. Kleppman was out of town, but they talked to his staff and to as many of her friends as they could find. The girls said they hadn't known Celeste very well. But if they didn't know much about her, they knew a lot about Kleppman's parties. Eventually, they agreed to testify before a grand jury. Described in the press as "skinny", "willowy" and "beautiful ", they testified that Mary Louise had approached them at shopping malls and community colleges, Olive Garden restaurants and trailer parks and told them they could make two hundred dollars if they took their clothes off to massage wealthy naked men.

Kleppman's lawyers challenged the girls' credibility. One of the girls had behavior problems, they said, and lived during the week at an "involuntary-admitted juvenile educational facility." Another girl had been arrested for shoplifting a turquoise camisole from Victoria's Secret. A third girl had been involved in an extortion ring, luring men into public washrooms at City Place and the Gardens Mall to have sex while an accomplice secretly recorded their encounters. Three days before she appeared before the grand jury, Kleppman's lawyers sent private investigators to harass the family of a fourteen-year-old girl and threaten them with deportation if they allowed her to testify. Another girl said Mary Louise had contacted her by phone and told her that Kleppman would compensate girls who supported him but find ways to deal with any girl who went against him. In return for their silence, Kleppman referred some of the girls to the modeling agency that he co-owned with a man named Paco.

Kleppman's house manager, one of his maids and the groundskeeper all testified before the grand jury but then recanted their testimony and said they'd forgotten many of the details of that night. The police were skeptical, but they could do nothing. After his convenient lapse of memory, the house manager, whose name was Evan, retired to a small bungalow in Jacksonville, Florida, and spent six months of the year with his wife in Aruba in a house owned by Kleppman's friend Hamilton Roebuck.

Since the case against Kleppman depended on the stories of a few adolescent girls with bad reputations, all of us were surprised when the Florida state prosecutor charged him with six counts of statutory rape and two counts of soliciting. Even The Palm Beach Spectator carried a story about the case, although we focused most of our attention on the theft of the jeweled lizard from Villa Patrizia. Other news outlets weren't so circumspect, but without hard information from credible sources they soon moved on to feed their readers' appetites for more salacious stories.

Kleppman's friends like Leonard Friesen didn't let the matter drop so easily. Men like Friesen paid Kleppman to handle their money, to scrub it clean and give it back to them in nice neat bundles of legitimate wealth, and they expected him to do it discreetly. They didn't like to see Kleppman's name in the news. Sooner or later some enterprising reporter would connect the dots that led from Kleppman to them. An insurance adjuster had already contacted Leonard Friesen to ask him questions about the jeweled lizard he'd bought at Melanie Merriwether's auction. Leonard valued his privacy. He didn't like it when strangers started snooping around in his business.

Most of us spend time with friends because we like them and our positive feelings go beyond the limitations of expedience. But people like Kleppman and Friesen don't have friends, they have contacts. They measure the quality of a relationship by one criterion: money. They assess a person's value by how much they can get from him. You or I might feel insulted if we knew that a person valued our friendship for the contribution we might make to his bank account. But Kleppman's friends didn't feel that way at all. On the contrary, they felt flattered that such a wealthy man would accommodate them in his life. They were dazzled by Kleppman's wealth and blind to his motives. They felt privileged to speak about Kleppman as if he were a friend, and when they spoke about him, they never failed to mention his jet or his homes in Mayfair and Manhattan or his palatial vacation property in Palm Beach. To them, he wasn't just a man named Keith Kleppman; he was Keith Kleppman, the guy with all the money.

It took more than a year for Kleppman's case to wind its way into court, and by the time it did, he'd devoted himself to salvaging his reputation. For two thousand dollars an hour, he paid a public-relations consultant to portray him as the victim of a frame-up by a few teen-aged gold-diggers who'd offered their story to an over-zealous, politically ambitious prosecuting attorney. According to articles judiciously placed with compliant magazine editors, the prosecutor was trying to build his career on the back of a dedicated but misunderstood financial visionary. Under the headline "Hard-earned home time: A titan relaxes", Forbes magazine carried a picture of Keith Kleppman, in a polo shirt and khakis, lounging with his Irish water dog in the library of his brownstone on East 87th. In the photograph, Kleppman had his half-glasses on the end of his nose as if he'd just glanced up from the four-hundred-year-old folio in his hands of Shakespeare's Henry the Fourth, Part One, which he'd purchased for three million dollars from an antiquarian book dealer in London, although a close observer would have seen that he held it upside down.

The writer of the article dismissed the idea that a man of Kleppman's intellect, social standing and accomplishments would consort with disreputable low-lifes and morally questionable gold-diggers in Palm Beach. Referring to the Gettys, the Bronfmans and the Lamperts, the writer observed how great wealth attracts attention from opportunistic extortionists. She pointed out that Kleppman earned a salary of twenty-four million dollars a year, and his bonus the previous year had amounted to another sixty-four million, implying, I suppose, that he could afford to pay for a higher class of hooker than an opportunistic teenager from West Palm Beach. The article didn't mention that Kleppman's bonus was based mainly on sales of securities purchased by gormless state and municipal pension fund administrators or that his company had made another killing by shorting the securities while the pension funds hemorrhaged money, leaving their members with no retirement savings. All that would come out later.

Lauded for his astute financial mind, Kleppman, through his publicists, drew attention to his role as a director of the Securities Industry Association, chair of its Trading Committee and membership on the board of the International Securities Clearing Corporation in London. In interviews, Kleppman referred often to Moira Dunfield, chair of the Securities and Exchange Commission, as a "dear friend" and said SEC Commissioner Margaret Foster was a "terrific lady" whom he knew "pretty well." He also pointed out that he served on the boards of several nonprofit institutions, whose managers entrusted him with their endowments.

Through the Kleppman Family Foundation, he gave almost thirty million dollars to hospitals, theaters, educational, cultural, and health charities, an impressive sum until you realized that it represented less than four months' income. He also donated tens of thousands to Republican Senatorial campaigns, had his photo taken with three former U.S. presidents and with his friend Al Gore, the former vice-president, at an international conclave, where men with gigantic egos and cultivated gravitas read long-wind-ed speeches in ponderous tones about the necessity of compassion for the world's poor and hungry, before they retired to a private dining room at the Four Seasons for lunch.

Kleppman even practised being kind to his household staff, office cleaners and chambermaids just to make sure he could do it when he had to. But kindness didn't come naturally to him, and it made him feel vulnerable. He wouldn't have bothered if it hadn't furthered his ambitions. In private, where kindness didn't matter, he didn't bother with it at all. He continued to treat his staff as if they were human appliances. He might have paid them well and made a show of giving them gifts at Christmas, but all of them knew that, whenever their employer looked at them, he was thinking, "My great-grandfather owned your ancestors." The wife of the Kleppman's house manager told me she'd cleaned his house and shopped for him for six years and had never had a direct conversation with him. Kleppman made it clear, she said, that he did not want her to interact with him or even look at him when he was in the house. On one occasion, she said, when she remarked on the unseasonably cold weather, Kleppman went into a rage and ordered the woman out of the room.

Amazingly, none of this stopped Kleppman from indulging his appetites. If anything, it stimulated his hunger for girls and drugs and two-day parties. He seemed to think he was above the law, that he could buy his way out of trouble.

As Kleppman's trial date approached, some of his clients worried that he might lose his money, and the bond that held his friendships together began to crumble. Leonard Friesen was the first to withdraw his investments from KKIS. "Strictly business," he said to Kleppman. "Nothing personal." But they never spoke to each other again.

Some people said Friesen had acted too hastily. They had confidence that Kleppman would protect their investments. When I talked to Oscar Hornbeam at a charity gala at the Kravis Center, he said he admired Kleppman's courage under fire, his withering rebuttal of his critics "and his Bentley." In New York, he said, he and some of Kleppman's golfing buddies from Palm Beach had sent gifts during the trial to Kleppman's brownstone on the Upper East side: baskets of imported delicacies from Katz's Deli and amusing knick-knacks from Tiffany's, including a sterling silver polar bear lolling on a plinth engraved with the motto "Don't let the bastards get you down."

"I don't know how he stands it," said Suzy Hornbeam.

"The pressure must be immense," Oscar agreed.

"He'll get through it," said Benjamin Whittaker.

"Does he still have his money?" said Bibi.

"Of course he does," said her husband. "He's a smart businessman."

"I heard he's trying to sell his Brancusi," said Suzy Hornbeam.

"Darius says he's reconfiguring his collection," said Bibi.

"It's so unfair," said Suzy.

"As if he's to blame for all the suffering in the world," said Oscar.

"They don't know what it's like to have money," said Suzy. "They think it's easy."

"Give these people a million dollars, and they wouldn't know what to do with it," said Benjamin Whittaker. "Let them move to North Korea, I say."

"Where everyone's equal," said Oscar.

"Equally poor," said Bibi.

By the time Kleppman's case went to court, the public regarded him as the victim of a coven of scheming teen-aged vultures who had tried to take advantage of his status as a wealthy investor, philanthropist and defender of global harmony. The most persuasive testimony in the trial came from Mary Louise Hobsbawn, who had moved with Kleppman's help to New York to begin her modeling career with Paco's agency. She appeared in the courtroom with dark hair, wearing a conservative blazer and skirt. She admitted to arranging for Kleppman's accusers to come to his house, but she said they'd come to spend the night at her pyjama party. When Kleppman's attorney asked why Keith Kleppman would allow her to invite her friends to sleep over at his house, she said, "Why wouldn't he? He's been a friend of my father's since I was born. My father's a minister. And he's my Uncle Keith."

Upon his acquittal, Kleppman held a party at Mar-a-Lago with Hamilton Roebuck, Cyrus Beltran, Henry Kissinger, Donald Trump and other luminaries in the arts, entertainment and business worlds. Then he flew on his Gulfstream to Manhattan with three tall teenaged girls from Paco's modeling agency.

Even after being cleared of the charges against him, Kleppman continued the calculated philanthropic gestures that had drawn so much attention to his generosity. He endowed a cardiology unit at the Cornell Medical Center in New York and provided the money for two other research centers at universities in Philadelphia and Chicago, all of which bore his name in prominent gold letters over the front door. At Harvard, he established the Kleppman Center for Corporate Governance, although many members of the faculty regarded the gesture with disdain and dismissed the administrators of Harvard's business school as shills for a glorified vocational training program. In Georgia, the Atlanta Institute of Art had no reservations about accepting Kleppman's money to fund the G. Keith Kleppman Wing, which now accommodates the museum's pre-Columbian sculpture collection.

Through the Bishop of the Palm Beach Diocese, Kleppman donated a million dollars to the Catholic Church and sponsored a children's baseball league in Port St. Lucie. For opening his purse strings, he and several of his friends received a private audience with the Pope, with whom Kleppman discussed world poverty and the role of the church in providing solace to the poor.

"I've never seen so many people," said Suzy Hornbeam, when they returned home from the Vatican. "Lined up in the hot sun. They stand there for hours just to get a glimpse of the Pope. We went in through a side door. Thank God."

Two

One evening after he got home from work, Dwayne Forbes watched a black Dodge RAM pickup truck stop in front of his rented house on North K Street. The driver took his briefcase from the passenger seat and walked in his dress shoes across the hard sedge lawn. He was wearing a grey suit, a white shirt and a green and yellow striped tie. Dwayne thought the man might be a Jehovah's Witness, coming to talk to him about God and redemption. But Witnesses usually canvassed a neighborhood in pairs. He wondered if the man's partner was sick.

When Dwayne opened the door, the man held up an ID card and identified himself as Ed Fiko, "with a k." Then he said, "Not that you need to know how to spell my name."

"Where'd you say you're from?" Dwayne said.

"Chubb," said Ed Fiko. He held up the ID card again.

"Chubb?" said Dwayne.

"The insurance company?"

"You here about car insurance?" said Dwayne. He wondered if his Canadian policy covered him in the States.

"No," said Ed. "A robbery."

"Not sure if I can help you there."

Ed Fiko looked about the same age as Dwayne, but Dwayne was well over six feet tall, with smooth, soft features and fair hair, like a peach, while Ed was short and stocky, and his neck rose in a thick column from the collar of his shirt to his ears. His closely trimmed black hair against his white scalp reminded Dwayne of pepper sprinkled on a sheet of paper.

Dwayne invited him into the house and asked if he'd like coffee. "Sure," said Ed. "Two sugars, no cream."

"That's good," said Dwayne. "I don't have cream."

Ed sat down at the kitchen table and watched Dwayne as he filled the kettle and plugged it into the wall outlet beside the sink.

"Been here long, Dwayne?" said Ed.

"More than a year, now," Dwayne said. He said he'd come to Florida from Canada. He was going to explain that he'd settled on North K Street because of the palm trees, but changed his mind when he looked at Ed.

"How about yourself?" he said.

While Dwayne took cups from the cupboard, Ed said he'd graduated three years earlier from Florida State, in Tallahassee, where he'd played defensive tackle on the football team. He said he'd intended to go back to school to study microbiology, but he'd recently married his girlfriend. They had one child, with another on the way, and he'd put his plans on hold. "At least till the kids are older," he said. "So I got this job with Chubb. My uncle knew a guy. Kids aren't cheap."

"Tell me about it," said Dwayne. "So, somebody get robbed?"

Ed opened his briefcase and pulled out a glossy booklet with a photograph on the cover of Dwayne's lizard encrusted with jewels. Dwayne leafed through the pages, glancing at a sentence or two and the photo of his lizard and then looked more closely at the back page, where he studied a head shot of his half-brother, Mike.

"What the fuck?" he said.

Ed pointed at the cover. "That your lizard?" he said.

"Sure is," said Dwayne. "That's my lizard, all right. It's the rest of this stuff."

"How so?" said Ed.

Dwayne tapped his finger on the artist's head shot. "This guy, Michel Rondelle. That's my brother. Half-brother, actually. Name's Mike.

"But, look. He never lived on an Indian reserve. He never took art classes. The only thing he did was go to prison. Who wrote this thing? Juan Muñoz? Where'd you get this?"

"I'm not at liberty to say," said Ed.

"Was it Mary Louise?"

Ed shook his head. "Sorry. I can't tell you that."

Dwayne tapped the photo on the cover. "She got me to dress up this lizard. Not sure I should've done that."

"Why not?" said Ed.

Dwayne shrugged. "Didn't feel right," he said. "Hang on. I'll show you."

He went into the living room and came back with an unadorned wooden sculpture of a lizard.

"So you're an artist, too?" Ed said.

"I don't call myself an artist," said Dwayne.

134

"But you made this?"

"Yes, sir."

Ed ran his fingers over the wood. "Nice," he said. "How much?"

"You mean how much did I spend or how much do I sell it for?"

"How much do you sell it for?"

"Ten bucks, sometimes. I sell them at the flea market, over on the Dixie Highway."

"Business good?" said Ed.

"It's OK," said Dwayne. "I don't do it for money."

Ed raised his eyebrows and looked at Dwayne as if he was either a liar or a kook. "Why do you do it?" said Ed.

"Been doing it all my life," said Dwayne. "It's what I do, you know?"

"How old are you?" said Ed.

"Twenty-five."

"So not that long," said Ed.

"About as long as you've played football," said Dwayne. "Except you don't do that anymore."

"This one in the picture. With the jewels?" said Ed. "You know how much it's worth?"

"A woman paid me ten bucks for it," Dwayne said. "Before the jewels."

"Know who she was?"

"Like I said. Her name's Mary Louise Hobsbawn. Said she wanted jewels." Dwayne blushed. "You know what it's like. You meet a woman sometimes, you do things you don't want to do."

"Tell me about it," said Ed. "I should be studying bugs. Not that I'm complaining." He nodded toward the photo of the jeweled lizard in the glossy booklet. "Know how much that one's worth?"

"I can't say," said Dwayne.

"Take a guess," said Ed.

"I've never been good with money," said Dwayne.

"Give it a try."

"I don't like putting a price on my work."

"Just try," said Ed. "How much do you think it's worth?"

Ed's persistence began to irritate Dwayne. "How much is it worth?" he said. "I don't fucking know. How much would you sell your son for, you know? How much would you pay for a human life? Is it priceless? Worthless? I've heard that our bodies contain chemicals worth about two dollars. You think that's fair?"

"Let me rephrase the question," Ed said. "How much do you think someone paid for it?"

"No idea," said Dwayne. "Sorry. I don't like talking about money."

"Take a guess," said Ed.

"More than ten bucks, probably," said Dwayne. "Because of the jewels."

"A hundred thousand," said Ed. "Guy named Kleppman bought it."

"No way," said Dwayne.

"I'm serious," said Ed.

"Whoa," said Dwayne. "No shit."

"No shit," said Ed. "And somebody stole it."

"A hundred thousand." Dwayne shook his head. "You could buy a house."

"Art's a funny business," said Ed. "So we're looking into it. Probably nothing to do with you, but just in case."

He handed Dwayne a business card. He picked up the lizard from the table. "I should get one of these for my wife," he said. "Ten bucks?"

"The big ones are more," Dwayne said.

Ed took his wallet from his inside pocket and fished out ten dollars. "You got any more?" he said. "With jewels?"

Dwayne shook his head. "Like I said. I won't do that again."

"Even for a hundred thousand dollars?" Ed said.

Dwayne shrugged. "Nah," he said. "It's not the money."

"So why not?" said Ed.

Dwayne thought of the feeling he got when he worked on a sculpture, revealing with patience and infinitesimal care the spirit within a piece of wood. It was the closest he ever came to feeling love, and he deeply regretted betraying that feeling to win the affection of Mary Louise Hobsbawn. He thought of his mother, his dead father, his stepfather, Mary Louise, Darius Pierre. In one way or another, all of them had fallen short of their promise. All of them had let him down. Perhaps that was why people believed in God, to compensate for the shortcomings of all the disappointing people in the world who offered more than they delivered.

"Let me put it this way," said Dwayne. "You ever see a lizard wearing jewellery?"

Three

Ed Fiko didn't like to waste his time thinking about the clothes he wore. At the apartment in Coral Springs where he lived with his wife and son, he kept three identical suits, shirts and ties so he'd never have to worry about matching his wardrobe. The next morning around eleven o'clock, when he walked into the M2 Gallery carrying a briefcase in one hand and, in the other, Dwayne's lizard in a shopping bag, he wore a grey suit, a white shirt and a green and yellow striped tie, but not the same ones as he'd worn the day before when he'd visited Dwayne. When he found Darius at the back of the gallery, he held up an ID and identified himself, as he always did, as Ed Fiko, "with a k", from Chubb Insurance. "Not that you need to know," he said, but Darius didn't wait for him to say more.

"I don't need insurance," Darius said.

Ed said he had some questions about the theft of a sculpture. A lizard, by Michel Rondelle, he said. He placed his briefcase on the table. He opened it and pulled out the glossy booklet about the artist and his work. He pointed to the photograph of the jeweled lizard. "Our client filed a claim for a hundred and fifty thousand dollars," he said. "That right?"

"Sounds about right," said Darius. He sipped from a China coffee cup. He didn't ask Ed if he wanted coffee.

"So let's get this straight," Ed said. "People pay you to find pieces of art. You're like an agent, right?"

"Advisor," said Darius.

"And when you find a piece they like, you get a commission, am I right?"

"That's correct."

"So in this case, with this lizard, Michel Rondelle's lizard. The owner paid a hundred thousand for it, am I right?"

"That's correct," said Darius. He was growing impatient with this conversation. Ed Fiko belonged to the lumpen mass of insensitive people who understood nothing about art. Darius folded his arms across his chest. To-day he was wearing a silk shirt from Versace, emblazoned in gold with patterns of cowboy boots and spurs, under a Tom Ford leather jacket that cost more than Ed Fiko's truck.

"So you get a commission on a hundred thousand dollars."

"That's not correct. You obviously don't know much about the art market."

"I'm still learning," said Ed.

"I donated the sculpture. For charity."

"You bought it for ten dollars," said Ed.

"I didn't say that."

"How much did you pay for it?"

"I can't tell you that."

"That's okay," said Ed. "I understand. Privacy and all that."

"Whatever." Darius shrugged.

"Then you gave it to a charity, and someone bought it for a hundred thousand. You get a tax write-off for that?"

"Maybe," said Darius. "I haven't checked."

"So the buyer gets this lizard."

"For a hundred thousand," said Darius.

"Insures it," said Ed.

"For its value."

"More than he paid, though," said Ed.

"You have to understand," Darius said. "There's only one of these. It's the only work of its kind. There will never be another one. It's rare. Its value can only go up."

"Okay," said Ed. "Got it. But then it gets stolen."

"Which is why it was insured," said Darius.

Ed pulled the lizard from the plastic shopping bag and placed it on the table. "It was like this one," he said, watching Darius's face, "right?"

"Where did you get that?" said Darius.

"Guy named Dwayne Forbes," Ed said. "For ten dollars."

Darius picked up the lizard. "This one's different," said Darius.

"Why is that?" said Ed.

"No jewels."

"Okay, I see that."

Darius turned it over. "No signature," he said. "It's a fake."

"And those things – the jewels, the signature – would account for the difference? Ninety-nine thousand, nine-hundred-and-ninety-dollars?" said Ed. "For jewels."

"And a signature, yes."

"That's a big difference, don't you think?"

Ed's tone seemed to insinuate that he'd done something wrong.

"Listen, Mister Fiko, with a k," Darius said, "if I can buy something for ten dollars and sell it for a hundred thousand, that makes me a pretty sharp businessman. Wouldn't you say?"

"You could say that," Ed said.

"How would you describe it?" said Darius.

"Sounds to me like tax evasion," Ed said, "or money laundering, maybe. Something fishy."

"If that was the case," said Darius, "and I'm not saying it is, what business is it of yours?"

"None of my business," said Ed. "Insurance is my business."

"Where's my umbrella when I need it?" said Darius.

Ed rubbed his hand over the black bristles on his head. "I don't follow," he said.

"Surely you've heard that old chestnut," said Darius. "Insurance companies. Banks. You're all the same. Happy to sell umbrellas when it isn't raining."

Ed Fiko shook his head. "I'm missing something."

"You'll figure it out," said Darius.

Ed tapped his finger on the lizard on the table. "How much to turn that —" He held up the glossy booklet and tapped on the photo of the jeweled lizard – "into this?"

"No idea," said Darius. "You'd have to ask the artist."

"I did," said Ed.

"You talked to Michel Rondelle?"

"I talked to Dwayne Forbes. The guy who made this."

"And what did he say?"

"I'll tell you what he didn't say. He didn't say ninety-nine thousand, nine hundred and ninety dollars."

"That doesn't surprise me," said Darius.

"Why's that?" said Ed.

"Dwayne Forbes, whoever he is, isn't an artist."

"He said that, too," said Ed.

"Anything else?" said Darius.

"He said he wasn't in it for the money."

"Probably a good thing," said Darius.

"Why's that?"

"Someone who didn't know better might think it was a genuine Rondelle.

Happens all the time. People pay a lot of money. Turns out to be a fake."

"We wouldn't want that," said Ed.

"No," said Darius.

"One more thing," said Ed.

"What's that?"

Ed pointed again at the brochure. "At the moment, we've got only one of these lizards."

"Someone has it," said Darius.

"And we're looking for it," said Ed. "Believe me. Maybe we'll find it. Maybe we won't. If we find it, we'll give it back to Mister Kleppman."

"And if you don't find it?" said Darius.

"It's not so simple," said Ed.

"What's the complication?"

Ed picked up the lizard from the table. "I have this lizard here, worth ten dollars."

"The price that your friend charges," said Darius.

"Not really my friend," said Ed. "But he made this."

"It could be worth more," said Darius. "An artist is the last person to know what his work is actually worth."

"Okay," said Ed. "But at the moment, it's not. And here's the thing. Dwayne Forbes has more than one of these plain lizards." He tapped again on the brochure. "This one? Supposed to be worth a hundred thousand? There's only one."

"There's only one Mona Lisa," said Darius.

"The Mona Lisa has a track record," said Ed. "Whatever you call it. Provenance. It's been bought and sold. And people have paid good money for other stuff that Rembrandt did."

"Da Vinci," said Darius.

"Right," said Ed. "Da Vinci. He has a track record, is what I'm saying. This guy Michel Rondelle? Nobody's ever heard of him."

"This brochure says otherwise," Darius said.

"That could be," said Ed. "But so far, I can't find anything else that Michel Rondelle has sold for anywhere close to a hundred thousand dollars."

"Sometimes an artist doesn't sell until he's dead," said Darius.

"Oh my heavens," said Ed. The words sounded quaint coming from the mouth of a man shaped like a fire hydrant. "Let's hope that doesn't happen."

"The point is," said Darius, "your company won't honor its policy."

"I'm saying we have a lizard by Michel Rondelle." Ed tapped his finger on the brochure. "Worth a hundred thousand."

"Hundred and fifty," said Darius.

"Right," said Ed. "He tapped the lizard on the table. "And we have this one. Sells for ten dollars. And there's more where it came from."

Darius scowled. "Umbrellas," he said. He stood up.

"What about 'em?" said Ed.

"Wait till it rains," said Darius.

Four

Dwayne was surprised when he answered a knock at the door that afternoon after work and found Darius Pierre standing outside dressed in tennis shoes, khaki pants and a navy-blue polo shirt. The Aston Martin was parked in the driveway behind Dwayne's pickup truck.

Dwayne held the door open and invited him inside. Darius shook his head.

"I can't stay long," he said. "I just thought I should warn you."

"About what?" said Dwayne.

"Your brother," said Darius.

"What's he done now?"

"He's reported you to immigration. He knows you're in this country illegally."

"Fuck," said Dwayne. "I can't believe it. Actually, I can believe it. Nothing surprises me about my brother."

"You should do whatever you want to do," said Darius, "but if I were you, I'd leave as soon as you can."

"I have a job," said Dwayne.

"That's part of the problem," said Darius. "You're not supposed to have a job."

"I can't just leave."

"It's better if you do," said Darius.

"I have to go to work tomorrow."

"You probably shouldn't do that," said Darius.

"I can at least get paid," Dwayne said.

"It's not just you who could get in trouble. The company you work for, they could get in trouble, too."

"I'm not sure I have enough money to leave," said Dwayne, thinking of the empty paper bag in the vegetable drawer.

"Maybe I can help you out," said Darius. He pulled a wad of cash from his pocket.

"That's okay," said Dwayne. He felt reluctant to accept charity from a stranger.

"It's not a gift," said Darius.

"What can I give you in return?"

"How about those sculptures?"

"My carvings?" said Dwayne.

"Sure," said Darius. "How many do you have?"

"I don't know," said Dwayne. "Fifteen. Twenty."

"I'll give you four hundred dollars for them. Make it five. How's that sound?"

Dwayne watched as he peeled a few bills from the bundle in his hand.

"That should get you back to Canada," Darius said.

Dwayne went inside then and returned a couple of minutes later with his carvings in five plastic shopping bags. They didn't weigh much. He and Darius carried them to the car.

"You've got my card," Darius said. "But here's another one. Call me when you get home."

Dwayne looked up and down the street. "I'm gonna miss this place," he said.

"You can always come back," said Darius.

Darius got into the car, drove away from the house and turned the corner. When he was out of sight, he stopped by the curb, dialed the number of the Homeland Security tip line and left the address of the house on North K Street.

A week later, the landlord came from his car dealership to collect the overdue rent from Dwayne. When no one answered the door, he let himself in. He could tell as soon as he entered the house that Dwayne had moved out. The landlord had dealt enough times with tenants who skipped out on their rent to recognize the signs of an abandoned property. The doors and windows had been closed for so long, the air inside the house had gone stale. The walls no longer throbbed with a human presence but seemed to reflect emptiness. The floors creaked before he stepped on them. The cupboards were bare and the refrigerator was empty, although Dwayne had cleaned the house thoroughly before he left.

The landlord walked through the house, checking the bathroom and the bedroom for damage. He returned to the kitchen on his way to the front door when he noticed a small jewellery box on the counter. There was nothing to indicate that it had been left deliberately for him. But Dwayne had removed everything else from the house, leaving not even a scrap of paper on the floor or a coat hanger in the closet, and he'd left the place as clean as the day he arrived. He must have known that the landlord would come to inspect the empty house and would find the box. He didn't recognize the name of the shop, Kaufmann de Suisse, which was printed in gold lettering on the lid. Inside, he found a gold bracelet studded with rubies and sapphires. There was a note inside, written to someone named Mary Louise. There was no address on the box and the landlord had no way of tracking down the woman. He took the box away with him. He waited for almost two weeks, but when he didn't hear from Dwayne, he wrapped the box as a gift and gave it to his wife. She was overcome with emotion and asked why he'd given her such an expensive piece of jewellery. "Just because I love you," he said.

Five

Darius used the car's GPS to drive to The Church of the Lord Jesus. He'd been there several times, but if he tried to follow the route from memory, he drove down dead-end streets or sailed along the South Dixie Highway looking for an intersection that would take him to Johnson Street even as he looked across a field of scrub and litter at the church where he wanted to go. The GPS helped, but he found all the right- and left-hand turns frustrating, and when he got there he hated to leave his car parked outside the church in case it was vandalized. To hear him talk, you'd have thought he'd driven into a war zone in Damascus.

He took the sculptures in five plastic bags from the car and carried them to the front door of the church. He wasn't surprised to see that a vandal had used a black magic marker to draw a penis on the white paint and scribbled the word SUCK underneath it. The word reminded Darius of Mary Louise's T-shirt. He tried the door, but it was locked. He followed a gravel path to a door at the side of the building. When he turned the handle, it opened into a small hallway. Carrying the five plastic bags, he found Pastor Bob at his desk in the converted bedroom that he used as an office. He was in his shirtsleeves with his pant legs rolled up, bathing his feet in two plastic buckets of water.

"Epsom salts," said Pastor Bob. "Good for the aches and pains, my friend. Have to do something. I'm on my feet all day. Have a seat."

He nodded at a kitchen chair on the other side of the desk. Darius noticed a scruffy white dog curled up in Pastor Bob's lap. The pastor reached for a pack of Kool cigarettes, lit one, leaned his enormous head over the back of his chair and blew smoke rings toward the ceiling. "What can I do for you?" he said.

Darius put the bags down on the floor. "I need a place to store these," he said.

"What you got there?" said Pastor Bob.

"Sculptures," said Darius. "Lizards."

"More fucking lizards," said Pastor Bob.

"I thought you liked lizards," said Darius.

"Live ones, maybe," said Pastor Bob.

Darius held up one of the wooden lizards. "These don't bite," he said.

"What happened to the jewels?" said Pastor Bob.

"These are fakes," said Darius. "No jewels."

"Why keep them here?" said Pastor Bob.

"I'm thinking about what to do with them."

"Well don't think for too long," said Pastor Bob.

"Why's that?" said Darius.

"I'm moving the church," said Pastor Bob. "Soon as Mary Louise starts making money. Should be any day now."

"You've heard from her?"

"Once or twice," said Pastor Bob. "She's busy. Being a model, most people think it's easy. You just stand around all day acting beautiful and letting some guy take your picture. Let me tell you, it ain't so easy. That's why she left her little mutt here for me to take care of. Models have no time for pets."

"And you should know," said Darius.

"It's what she says," said Pastor Bob.

"Anybody else know you've heard from her?"

"If they do, they didn't hear it from me," said Pastor Bob.

"Good," said Darius. "I'll tell Mister Kleppman."

Pastor Bob stubbed out his cigarette. He took a towel from the desk and spread it on the floor. He pulled his feet out of the buckets and positioned them on the towel.

"How much will it take?" said Darius.

"To store your lizards?" said Pastor Bob. He grunted as he leaned over to dry his feet.

"To build a new church."

"Fuck," said Pastor Bob. "How should I know? You talking from scratch?"

"New building. Better location. Yeah," said Darius. "From scratch."

"Christ," said Pastor Bob. "Fifty. Maybe a hundred thousand. Haven't really thought about it, tell you the truth."

"Think about it," said Darius. "You do me favors. I do you favors. Works out for both of us."

"Cicero," said Pastor Bob.

"What?"

146

"Latin guy. Writes about friendship. That's what we have here. A friendship."

"Let's see where we can put these," said Darius. He picked up the shopping bags.

Pastor Bob put the dog on the floor. His bare feet squeaked on the shiny tile floor as he led Darius down the hall to the sanctuary at the front of the building. He went over to the aquarium and looked inside. "Hello, Gracie," he said. Beside the aquarium there were two sculptures of lizards. Darius recognized the one that Mary Louise had bought from Dwayne at the flea market. He looked at the other one, saw the jewels and realized it was Kleppman's.

"How long have you had this one?" he said.

"Few months, maybe," said Pastor Bob. "Mary Louise brought it home. She's been gone now since February."

"She say where she got it?" said Darius.

"No idea," said Pastor Bob. "I like the other one better. That one she got for ten bucks. Probably paid more for this one, what with the glass chips and all."

"She tell you where she got it?"

"Same place as the other one, probably."

"She didn't say anything about it?"

"Something about insurance," said Pastor Bob.

"She was going to collect the insurance?" said Darius.

"No, more like she was keeping it for insurance. I wasn't really listening. My daughter doesn't make much sense at the best of times. She comes home from Kleppman's, she sounds like she's on another planet. Hell, she's fifteen. I don't ask."

He led Darius to a closet at the back of the room. "You can put those lizards in here," he said, holding the door open. Darius placed the bags on the floor.

Pastor Bob and Darius walked to the front door. Pastor Bob unlocked it. He and Darius shook hands. He looked at the mauve Aston Martin parked in the street. "Still got that fancy car," he said. "All that money. Never understood the attraction myself."

He stood for a moment, barefoot, with his pants rolled up, watching Darius get into the car. He listened as the engine started, watched Darius pull away from the curb, then turned around to go inside but stopped when he noticed the big penis drawn on the door. "Fuck," he muttered. He stepped inside. "There's people in this world . . "

He was about to close the door behind him when the dog darted outside.

"Jeff," he commanded. "Get the fuck in here."

Six

Early on a Thursday morning in late November, the artist named Michel Rondelle was at a club off Worth Avenue called Nino's. He'd just ordered two more bottles of cask-strength Balvenie for the house. Now he stood at the bar and, in a loud voice, drank a toast to Melanie Merriwether, who was sitting at a table near the side of the room, then one to Darius Pierre, his dealer, at the same table, another toast to Shirko, the coke dealer, at the end of the bar, and a few more to people in the bar whose names he didn't know but who had, over the course of the evening, become his best friends. Before each toast, he filled his glass to the brim and, after raising it in one slurred tribute after another, he emptied it again.

The artist had come to the bar a few hours earlier with Darius and Melanie to celebrate the sale of one of his sculptures. They'd started drinking wine, but after five hours, he wanted single malt. "Why the fuck not?" he said. He looked at Melanie. "It's on your tab, right?"

At this late hour, only a few people lingered in the club, but Michel Rondelle shared his Scotch with each of them, carrying a bottle from table to table to refill any that looked empty.

He could be amusing at times. People laughed when he asked Melanie in a loud voice from the bar why she preferred Darius to him, although they became uneasy when he prolonged the interrogation, grabbed his crotch and punctuated his outburst with lewd gyrations. They laughed again when he talked about his brother, the one who had all the advantages and all the luck and never had to do things the hard way, "the way I did, fuck sake, one wrong turn after another, one step forward." He stepped forward. "Two steps back." He stepped back and tripped over a chair behind him and would have fallen if Shirko hadn't grabbed his shoulders to keep him upright. "You gotta think like an artist," he said when he regained his footing. "That's what I told him. None of this nine-to-five shit. Not if you want to make it big, baby."

Darius called his name, gestured to him to come back to their table, but Michel Rondelle was on a roll. After three more straight shots he collapsed onto the floor. This time, Shirko couldn't catch him, and he slammed his skull against the brass foot rail "like Dylan Thomas," Rollo Barnes said later, "without the poetry."

And that's how this story began, and how it ends.

An autopsy revealed that Michel Rondelle had consumed much more than Scotch and red wine before he died. He'd also injected himself with cocaine and heroin, a combination called a speedball. A speedball supposedly killed another artist named Jean-Michel Basquiat.

As it had for Basquiat, death enhanced the reputation of Michel Rondelle. The next time a Rondelle sculpture came onto the market, it came from Melanie Merriwether's collection. It sold for two hundred thousand dollars, seventy five thousand dollars over the estimate.

From time to time a dealer tried to sell a sculpture that resembled a Rondelle, but without a certificate of authenticity and the artist's initials under the head, the work was dismissed as a probable fake, a conclusion confirmed by the expert in Rondelle's work, Darius Pierre. But once in a while you still might see one of these pieces at a flea market, where you can usually buy it for ten or fifteen dollars. Even the fakes look pretty good to me. But like I said, I don't know much about art. As Ed Fiko, the insurance adjuster, says, "Art's a funny business."

CPSIA information can be obtained
at www.ICGtesting.com
Printed in the USA
BVHW031546040221
599268BV00002B/153

9 781952 085048